The Secret Room

Marion Eames

GOMER

First published by Christopher Davies, 1975
New edition - Gomer Press, 1995

© Marion Eames

ISBN 185 902 291 X

This book is published with the support of the Arts Council of Wales

Printed by J.D. Lewis & Sons Ltd., Gomer Press, Llandysul, Dyfed

PART I

1

It was the year the singing and dancing returned to the Hiring Fair. The old men were reminded of their young days when Charles— God rest his soul—had been king, those days long before Oliver and his mob had banished laughter from the land.

You should have seen the great birch trees we used to carry on to the common at Dolgellau, they cried, and the Morris Dancers from Shrewsbury prancing around and waving their kerchieves. Then there was the cockfighting, and the biggest bear in the world, and the gentry down from Nannau and Hengwrt throwing pennies to the children. And though you might hardly credit it, the way we look now, we, too, could sing and dance the *Cadi Ha* with the best of them. Sad to think it had vanished for so long, all the dancing and the merriment.

And yet, said those who had journeyed beyond the border of Wales to Chester, things had been worse in England. Thank God the Puritans had made little headway this side of Wrexham, and scant welcome had there been for Oliver's men with their long faces and endless carping at innocent fun of honest men. But now at long last Oliver, the Lord Protector, and his unlamented son belonged to history. So, too, Morgan Llwyd and Maesygarnedd. Another Charles, the Merry Monarchs had been on the throne these twelve years past, a fine gentleman who knew how to enjoy himself and was for everyone else doing likewise. So in this year of Our Lord 1672 laughter was well and truly restored to the land.

As their feet tapped out the rhythm of the dance, the old men chuckled at the familiar words.

> *Up along, Cadi Ha,*
> *Morris Stout, oe'r the line go prancing,*
> *Up! There he goes.*
> *And tail of calf*
> *And tail of cow*
> *And tail of Richard Parry now*
> *Up! There he goes.*

The girls formed a circle around the dancing men. They clapped their hands, their red flannel petticoats awhirl as they swayed their bodies from side to side in time to the music. Now and again a dancer would break away and reach out at one of the girls. Screams of laughter would fill the air, drowning for the moment the repetitive scraping of Siôn the Fiddler.

On the outskirts of the crowd three men stood watching. Their dress set them apart from the others, yet it was obvious from the way they acknowledged greetings all around that they belonged to the neighbourhood. Each in his own way was aware of the attention he attracted.

One of them, considerably older than the other two, held his head high and spoke with a ringing authority, raising a silk handkerchief to his nose with an exaggerated gesture.

'A pity the peasants smell so. Otherwise I might have ventured a turn in the next dance.'

He nodded in the direction of a well-rounded young girl who had been eyeing him for some time.

'With her, for instance, hey Rowland?'

He gave the youngest of the three a suggestive dig in the ribs.

'Ah well, my chance will come no doubt. Who is she, Robin?'

Rowland looked troubled but Robin replied with a grin:

'Nans. From Goetre.'

It pleased Robert Lewis that he was able to name the girl who had attracted Hywel Vaughan's attention. He greatly admired the elegant man of fashion and wished to emulate him in every respect—in his dress, his presence, his wealth and in his way with women. Above all in his cool, disdainful manner. Knowing the girl put Robert, for a brief moment, on a level with Hywel.

Watching Nans, Rowland was suddenly reminded of Meg but immediately he felt ashamed. Meg with her black hair and dark eyes. How could he possibly compare her with that redhead?

In spite of himself, he continued to stare at the girl. Her lips—that was it. Lips as full as ripe strawberries. And there was something familiar in the way she held herself . . .

He tried to stop his thoughts running in this direction. What had made him associate his wife with that strumpet? The truth was that he was always thinking of Meg. There were ribbons for her in his pocket, and he caressed the soft silk with his fingers. She loved to dress in the latest fashion. And why not? Did she not come of excellent stock? And was she not the wife of the owner of Bryn Mawr? Suddenly he was tired of his companions and of the fair. He longed to be out of the town and on his way home.

'Our friend doesn't agree?"

Robert Lewis was sniggering and Rowland sensed rather than heard the nature of Hywel Vaughan's jibe. He forced himself to ask. 'Agree with what?'

'No matter. Hardly words for the ears of such a recent bridegroom.'

Not for the first time Rowland Ellis had doubts about Hywel Vaughan. True, he was good company when the mood took him and he could talk well and wittily, especially about London and other far-off places. Also, of course, he was a kinsman, albeit a distant one. But there was a quality about him which disturbed Rowland—a cynical, contemptuous attitude towards even his closest friends. He expected the worst of everyone and was glad when he was proved right. He had never been heard to speak well of a living soul.

Rowland drew his cloak about him more closely, feeling the first shiver of autumn blow down from Cader. The sun was almost setting. Soon, when he had seen Siôn Dafydd, the Drover, he could return home with his business at the fair completed.

Abruptly the dancing had stopped and the crowd began to saunter around, seeking new diversions. The three men stood uncertainly where they were for a moment. Suddenly a small hobgoblin of a man ran past them shouting excitedly.

'What did he say?' asked Hywel.

'I didn't hear him aright,' replied Robert Lewis. 'Something about an old witch in the river Wnion, I think.'

Hywel turned lazily to his companions.

'Heigh-ho, happy days are back, in truth. Observe the good clean fun of the common people. Singing, dancing, drinking and wenching—and if the sport palls and there's bitterness in the vine—let's try drowning a witch. We can't afford to miss this, I vow.'

Rowland said he must leave, but Hywel would have none of it.

'It will improve your education. In any case, you said you had to see the drover, Siôn Dafydd, before going home. That's where you'll find him, take my word for it, and right at the very front, I'll warrant.'

Rowland's heart sank. He hated these old customs when sport degenerated into something fearsome and primitive. But it was no use arguing with Hywel Vaughan, and it was true he wanted to see Siôn Dafydd. He might as well follow the others and then make his escape as soon as he could. He sensed Hywel watching him quizzically.

'You must learn to enjoy yourself in this world, Rowland. Time enough to be serious in the next, when the flames begin to lick at your feet.'

Near the bridge, over the Wnion, there was a deep pool. Here scolds and witches were locked into the dreaded Red Chair and lowered into the water. If the woman managed to keep her head above water, this was proof that her soul had surely left her body for the devil was looking after his own. If she sank below the surface, she was innocent. But all too often proof came too late to save her life.

By the time the three men reached the green a large crowd had already gathered. Hywel pushed his way through with the aid of his sword and the people fell back to make way for the Squire of Hengwrt. The raucous voices and lewd laughter of the rabble deafened Rowland. By sunset beer and mead would have had their effect.

He almost stumbled over the wooden leg of an old soldier whose drunken face leered into his own. A young woman tugged at his coat and screamed something unintelligible in his ear. She laughed hysterically as she let him go. Little boys from the town crept provocatively between the legs of the older people and no one heard their screams as they were trampled underfoot.

Suddenly, for an instant the crowd was silent—then, as if bidden by some unseen leader, the mob broke into loud cries: 'The witch. Here she is!'—'To the Wnion with the witch!'

Yelling, they made way for a cluster of youths who were dragging an old woman behind them. Fear had made her staring eyes round as an owl's. Her wrinkled mouth, open wide in a scream, revealed one yellow fang of a tooth. Her grey hair hung in greasy knots over her shrunken shoulders. Desperately she tried to pull the remnants of her tattered clothing over the exposed flesh of her old body, and a hoot of laughter went up as one of the men tore her shirt apart to reveal her yellow, sagging breasts.

Rowland was sickened by the sight. He turned his head to look for Siôn Dafydd so that he could finish his business and escape.

At last he saw him—standing by the pool brandishing his whip. He was very drunk and bawling at the top of his voice.

'Come here, you—you skinny old crone. We'll see who's your master, by damn!'

He lashed the surface of the water wildly with his whip, wetting everyone within reach, while bystanders laughed and shouted their encouragement.

'Siôn Dafydd, the drover, for judge!'

'Forward the prisoner.'

'Come on, Siôn!' urged the men around him. 'Tell us if Betsan Prys is guilty or not.'

The old woman was thrust forward to stand shivering before the drover, who stared at her drunkenly, his flabby lips shining in his fat, red face.

'W-what is the charge?' he asked thickly, cracking his whip to another roar of laughter from the crowd.

A voice answered him: 'Bewitching the cows at Tynmynydd and making them dry.'

Other voices joined in: 'Dancing naked with the devil last Michaelmas!'

'She refused to go to church.'

'She poisoned Thomas Caerau's turnips.'

Siôn Dafydd raised his hand for silence.

'B-Betsan Prys,' he said, pointing his whip at the woman's face. 'You heard th-those ser-ious charges? What say you, hey?'

Betsan opened her mouth, but this time it was not to scream.

Instead the crowd heard a softly-hissed, malevolent curse that struck terror in their hearts. There was no mistaking it. She had cursed Siôn Dafydd, the drover. The noisy laughter dwindled into uneasy silence. Siôn Dafydd fell back a step as if reeling from a blow. Some of the onlookers swiftly and secretly crossed themselves.

Gradually a murmur rose among them, spreading like a wind through the rushes. It became louder and louder like the approaching baying of blood-thirsty hounds. If previously some of them had felt compassion for Betsan Prys, they dared not show it now. She was doomed.

The young men heaved her up and held her high, a screaming, protesting bundle of rags. Then, not waiting to put her in the Red Chair, they flung her like a rat into the middle of the pool. The crowd, satisfied, pressed forward eagerly to watch her fate.

'She's sinking!'

A loud cry of disappointment greeted these words, but another cry quickly followed.

'No. No. There she is!'

'Once again!'

Rowland could stand it no longer. He tried to reach the end of the pool but was hemmed in on all sides by the surging crowd.

'Far better leave things as they are.' He turned to discover that the quiet voice beside him belonged to Dr. Ellis, the Rector of Dolgellau. 'It's too late, in any case!'

Rowland knew the rector was right. How long, he wondered, did it take to drown a witch? He gazed with repugnance at the water where Betsan's face was appearing above the surface, her eyes closed, her mouth open.

He closed his own eyes and felt waves of nausea. He shivered. Dr. Ellis was still talking in his thin, scholarly voice.

'A pity the Fair should end thus,' he said. 'But that's how it is. None more cruel than an ignorant peasant full of fear.'

But what was there to fear in a poor old crone like Betsan? At first it had been little more than teasing. But when she had laid her curse on one of their company fear and hate had entered the game. Hatred always begat hatred.

Rowland looked at the spare frame and gentle, preoccupied eyes of Dr. Ellis and thought to ask him whether he was not at times troubled by the actions of some of his flock, but the good man had turned away and was already making for the solitude of the rectory, his thoughts on the Red Book of Hergest and the lives of the saints—and God knew what else.

One by one the candles spurted into life in the windows, and, as he made his way home, Rowland imagined they were stars from the heavens, fallen from grace. With every step he took out of the town away from the evil he had just witnessed, his spirits rose a little.

The leaves on the trees were changing to the mellow shades of autumn, but, as he reached Penybanc which lay at the top of the first steep hill out of the valley, the bronze tints had become blurred by the greyness of evening. Deeply breathing in the dampness of the earth and the scent of the fresh ferns, made sharp by the oncoming night, he looked down at Dolgellau and saw that it was shrouded in mist from the river Wnion, as if hiding its face in shame.

His business with Siôn Dafydd had been unfinished after all and he saw again the foolish grin and the saliva dripping from the drover's lips just as it did from the mouths of his own cattle. Betsan's screams still rang in his ears and he tried in vain to blot out the sight of her pathetic, shrivelled body.

Sitting on a hillock, he put his head in his hands, striving to shut everything out. He longed for peace, but it was no use. Wearily he rose to his feet and went on with his climb to Bryn Mawr.

It was getting late. Meg would be waiting impatiently for the ribbons—and maybe for him too. She hated missing the Fair. She was so fond of dancing—dancing and playing her harp. He could see her now, sitting on her three-legged stool, her silk skirts caressing the sound-board of the triple harp, her slender fingers made for tasks no coarser than plucking at harp strings, embroidering and making love.

This last month it had been difficult for her to sit comfortably at her harp at all, but it would all be over in time for the Flower Fair in April. What if Meg . . . ? A certain fear had nagged him since the moment she had told him the news. Was it possible for joy ever to be complete?

Perhaps Hywel, too, was haunted by doubts like these. Was that why he seized on each experience as it came, without counting the cost? As he thought of Hywel, the shadow of Betsan returned. He was thankful to see the gates of Bryn Mawr, and his heart lifted at the sight of the welcoming lamp in the window.

Meg lay on the bed, munching an apple, her third in an hour Pregnant women had these cravings, so they said, and in any case she had nothing else to do. Malan was preparing supper in time for

13

Rowland's return from the Fair. Siân Tynclawdd used to crave for strawberries and little Morgan had been born with a red mark on his hand. The mark always showed up at strawberry time. What if her child were born with a lump like an apple on his forehead or his chin?

Meg hastily dismissed the notion from her mind. She never allowed herself to dwell on uncomfortable thoughts. The sudden movement of the child within her excited her. At first it had frightened her, but now she waited for it with sensuous expectation.

She looked at her body with displeasure, weary of its shapelessness. The end of September, the apothecary had said. Her teeth closed over the apple and she bit into it noisily. A velvet gown would be nice after the child was born—blue velvet embroidered with cream lace, perhaps. Then she could go to Hengwrt and look every bit as fine as Lowri Vaughan and the wife of Corsygedol. If only she could persuade Rowland to move to a bigger place, one more worthy of their social position. Then they could entertain all the gentry around, and Rowland could become a Justice, and perhaps a Sheriff.

She shook the pillow impatiently. What hope had she of persuading him? He was stupid about Bryn Mawr. Meg aimed the apple core at the open window and missed, but did not bother to pick it up. She lay on her back and listened.

How quiet it was! Not a whisper—not even from the great oak, nor from the pine trees on the hill behind the house. The flame of the candle stood erect and still. She sat up suddenly, hearing footsteps on the narrow stony path. Rowland at last. She listened to the light, familiar step, the sound of the latch being lifted and the creak of the old oak door. Then came the eager call: 'Meg!'

A small, self-satisfied smile played around her lips. She let him call twice, and then slowly got up from the bed. She walked over to the mirror at the window and, like a cat after sleeping, stretched her body luxuriously, caressing her black ringlets as she pushed them back from her face.

Malan's voice came from the buttery.

'Is that you, master? The broth's ready.'

But Rowland was half way up the stairs.

'Meg! Are you all right?' he asked breathlessly.

She stood at the top of the stairs to greet him, holding a candle-stick in her hand.

'Don't be so nervous about me, Roli, of course I'm all right.'

She put the candle down on the chest nearby and twined her arms around her husband's neck. He caught her and hugged her tightly until she struggled for breath.

'Fie, Roli. How can I be all right if you go on like this?'

After a time, she asked in a small voice: 'Roli—did you get the ribbons?'

He straightened quickly and put his hand in his pocket.

'You didn't think I would forget, did you? Here, come to the light so that you can see them properly.'

'Red . . . and yellow . . . and white . . . and blue,' she breathed, holding the ribbons to the candlelight.

'Let me tie them in your hair . . . like this?'

'No, stupid. Not on my forehead!'

She ran happily back to her bedroom and gazed at herself in the mirror. She tried out the red ribbon a little above her ear, then tied it there.

'I've this for you, too!'

He drew from his other pocket a silk shawl of a texture so fine that it looked no more than a kerchief, until, like a magician, he shook the golden material out of its folds. As he placed the wrap on his wife's shoulders, she murmured: 'Oh, Roli . . . it's perfect!'

A lump rose in his throat as he looked at her. She was so close to him—and yet so far away. She seemed imprisoned by her own beauty. The candle-stick she held threw its light on the straight, slender nose, the marble white forehead, the delicate eyebrows like a swallow's wings and the black hair falling over her shoulders. At last she turned towards him.

'I am the Qu-e-e-en of Br-r-ryn Mawr!'

The house was filled with her laughter.

'The pregnant Queen!'

From the kitchen door old Malan watched the two of them descend the stairs, hand in hand. That's how it always was in the first years of marriage. Would it be the same at the end of five—or even sooner, wondered the old woman, remembering Guto Parri (as she did less often now) and how his loving had changed to bullying as soon as her figure had begun to lose its shapeliness.

Cadi, the young maidservant, was standing at the fireside ladling *llymru* from the boiling pot into bowls ready for setting on the long table in the middle of the kitchen. Benches flanked the table and a chair stood at either end. Rush lights threw long shadows across the room and the three-piece cupboard gleamed in the firelight. The servants stood at the benches waiting for the master and his wife to take their places. Rowland bowed his head as he said grace and, to the sound of benches scraping against the stone floor, the household sat down to supper.

In those days, Rowland Ellis employed three men servants and two maids at Bryn Mawr as befitted his position as a minor member of the squirearchy. Wales had made slow progress towards ridding itself of feudalism, but from the early years of the Civil War a new social order had begun to reveal itself, like a pattern slowly emerging on a tapestry.

Most Welsh people had remained loyal to the King during Cromwell's days, but the aristocracy had gradually lost their stranglehold on the country and new masters were appearing — the merchants and rich farmers.

For the first time it was possible for men of this class to become justices with power not only to run their own lives but those of other men as well. For the first time they had the right to question the authority of the King and of the Church. They learnt about William Harvey, about Galileo, and the scientific discoveries of the Royal Society. They were now able to read the Bible for themselves and to argue about its interpretation. Old ideas were giving way to new.

Rowland asked himself why he had been so deeply disturbed by what he had witnessed in the town that night. It had all happened before. But he realised he was no longer content to accept the old customs. Suddenly he was weighed down again by a sense of foreboding and his mood conveyed itself to the rest of the gathering around the table. They were unusually silent. Cadi was engrossed in her food. Malan's alert old eyes missed nothing and were troubled. The three farm-servants, old Dafydd, Huw Morris and Ellis, the lad from Penrhos, all kept glancing at their master from time to time. Meg alone seemed unaware of the gloom around her. She ate her food with relish and smiled a little as she fingered the new shawl on her shoulders.

16

Rowland had almost forgotten that this was Ellis's first night at Bryn Mawr. Observing the boy's thin face and his shyness, he smiled encouragingly at him.

'Welcome, Ellis Puw. I am rather late saying that, aren't I? You will be happy at Bryn Mawr with Dafydd. And Huw,' he added hastily, seeing Huw Morris's frown.

Ellis must be about sixteen. He had worked for seven years at Tyddyn-y-Garreg with Rowland's cousin, Lewis Owen. Knowing Lewis, Rowland was sure that the lad would be wellgrounded in farm work in spite of his youth. Lewis, himself a good farmer, demanded full value, and more, from his servants.

'Ellis Puw is a scholar, master.' Rowland saw how the boy flushed at the sarcasm in Huw Morris's voice.

'Oh, good,' he replied lightly.

But Huw was not for letting the matter rest there.

'You should see the books we have in our loft now. Like a priest's cell, it is.'

'Leave the boy alone,' growled old Dafydd.

Not for the first time did Rowland regret having hired Huw Morris for another season. Whenever the man opened his mouth the words struck like a serpent's tongue. But he was a good worker and physically in his prime. Even so, Rowland Ellis was unwilling to allow anyone to upset his household and it was obvious that the boy had already been harassed by Huw.

Meg laughed. 'Well, that's something new, for sure. Never before have we had a servant who could read. Who taught you, Ellis?'

The boy's flush deepened.

'Go on, tell your mistress, Ellis Puw,' goaded Huw.

'1 cannot,' the boy whispered, his eyes fixed on the bottom of his empty bowl.

'Come, come, Ellis Puw,' Meg's urging was kindly enough. She smiled at Huw. 'Why can't you tell me?'

'No, it is not that I can't tell you.'

The boy raised his eyes and looked directly at her.

'I cannot read, mistress.'

After a moment's silence, Meg looked around in mock astonishment. 'Well, upon my word, what's all the fuss about?'

'That's enough of this teasing.'

Rowland turned deliberately to Dafydd.

'Did you see anything of the fair, Dafydd Jones?'

The old man caught the hint.

'A little, master, but not much. As soon as the leaves begin to change colour, this rheumatism of mine turns up like an old friend, and the journey to town is beginning to tell on the old bellows by now, too.'

The conversation took a new turn and the boy looked gratefully at Rowland Ellis, but he knew he had not heard the last of Huw Morris's teasing.

The men were leaving the kitchen for their own quarters when Rowland Ellis called out to his new servant.

'Wait a moment.'

Ellis turned back, and Rowland said to Meg, 'Your pardon, my love. I'd like to have a word with Ellis on his own.'

Meg raised her eyebrows and her voice betrayed her displeasure. 'Oh, very well.'

'I shall not be long.'

He opened the door for her and, having closed it behind her, walked slowly towards the fireplace. Then he turned to the boy.

'Are you fond of books, Ellis Puw?'

'Yes, sir.'

'But you can't read.'

'Not—not yet, sir!'

'Have you any books?'

'Oh, yes, one or two.'

'Do you know what they are?'

'Oh, yes. Morgan Llwyd—the one about the birds talking. The *Beibl Bach*. And *Llyfr y Resolusion*.'

Rowland smiled. 'Not many who can read really understand those books.'

'No, sir, I don't quite understand them either. But if someone reads to me, somehow I can remember the words. And by repeating a passage to myself over and over, the meaning comes. I don't know whether it's the right meaning or not. But I'm learning to read that way, too.'

'Where did you get these books, Ellis Puw?' asked Rowland curiously.

The boy's face reddened again and his lips tightened uncharacteristically. 'I'm afraid I cannot tell you, Rowland Ellis.'

18

'Why not? No one need be ashamed of having books.'

He laughed but was suddenly struck with dismay. Surely the boy had not stolen the books? As if sensing Rowland's suspicions, Ellis Puw said quickly, 'There's nothing wrong, master. Only . . . only perhaps you wouldn't understand.'

'Very well then.' Rowland could see it was better to allow him to explain in his own good time . . . 'Tell me, what about the works of Morgan Llwyd? Do you know anything about him?'

'Oh, yes,' said the boy eagerly. 'He died about forty years ago. He was a famous preacher in the time of the Commonwealth. Don't you know about his work, master?'

'I've heard a little,' said Rowland cautiously.

'Listen to this passage. This is one I have come to understand through repeating it over and over again.'

He took a deep breath, fixed his eyes on the dresser behind Rowland and began to recite in a low, excited voice.

'There is need for neither Bible nor preacher. The true preacher stands in the pulpits of our hearts and the Book within us will serve if we follow it as the Word, or a Candle burning inside us in a dark place. Instead of hearkening to voices from without, we should follow the Light and obey the Voice that is within.'

Rowland Ellis felt cold. He could listen to no more. These were dangerous words, dangerous ideas. Did Ellis Puw realise this? He could hear Meg plucking at the strings of her harp and singing in a sweet, light voice.

'Why should I be sad,
Yes, why should I be sad,
Why should I be sad
And cast all joy aside?'

'Don't you feel a freedom, a kind of promise in those words, master? Don't you?'

The boy's eyes and the unnaturally red spot on each cheek reminded Rowland of his brother Guto during the early days of his consumption. He turned to speak lightly.

'Were those the words of Morgan Llwyd? More likely the ramblings of a Quaker. Take care, Ellis Puw, or you could find yourself following the Dolserau family into Caetanws jail.'

19

Ellis looked as if Rowland had struck him.

'I'm sorry. I thought . . . I heard that your father, Ellis Rees, in his day, sympathised with the Friends.'

Rowland noticed that the boy had used the original name for the strange sect that had earned the contemptuous title of 'Quaker'.

'My father was never one of those, Ellis Puw,' he said tersely. 'He once heard Vavasor Powell preach in Dolgellau many years ago, and that had some influence on him, but as for those extremists—oh, no.'

Ellis shifted from one foot to another, waiting uncomfortably for leave to go.

'That is all,' said Rowland curtly. Then suddenly he felt ashamed. 'No. Wait a minute. Would you like to learn to read?'

Rowland was not likely to forget the intensity in the swift reply. 'More than anything else in the world.'

Almost before he had had time to think, he heard himself say, 'Very well. We'll start our first lesson tomorrow night before bedtime. Bring your books down here.'

The boy's face showed his gratitude more eloquently than words. Rowland almost regretted his impetuous offer so great was Ellis's pleasure. Let's hope I have not started something that will prove to be a snare, he thought.

But what snare could there be in teaching a boy to read? He himself had been well educated. He might as well make use of his education this way. However, the uneasiness remained.

From the other room came the words of the song:

'I was young and happy,
Yes, so young and happy,
I was young and happy,
Make me so again.'

2

On Christmas Eve in the year 1672 Ann, the daughter of Rowland and Margaret Ellis, Brynmawr, was three months old and her mother proposed leaving her for the first time to go with her husband to the Plygain at Hengwrt. Rowland was none too happy about leaving the baby even in the care of the reliable old Malan, but he knew how much Meg had looked forward during the past six months to returning to a social life. Ever since the birth of the child she had talked of little else, so that Rowland had not the heart to object.

But it was still morning and there was plenty of work to be done before the time came to harness Barnabas and Ned ready for their ride through the town to Hengwrt. Rowland went out into the yard looking for Ellis Puw, who was to take a cartload of alder wood to the clogmaker. Mercifully, the weather was dry and not too cold, although the branches of the trees showed signs of hoar-frost.

Rowland paused to take in the beauty of the morning. How he loved his old home. It rose from a hill, as sturdy as Cader Idris in the background, a stone house built by his grandfather, Rhys Lewis, fifty years before. He marvelled always at the uniform shape of the stones the old man had gathered for his task and never ceased to wonder at the magnificence of the mountains in that part of Wales. Down towards Dolgellau and beyond, acre upon acre of pastureland fringed the mountain ranges of Moel Offrwm, Aran Mawddwy and Cader Idris. But that day Dolgellau was hidden from sight by a mist that lay on the town like a shroud.

Moel Offrwm glimmered in the distance and far away to the north east, Rhobell Fawr cast its shadow over the valleys. Towards the west where the sea rolled, the mountains of Diffwys rose, rich in gold, copper, manganese and who knows what other treasures?

The silvery frost stirred his imagination and he was filled with an almost painful love for this land of his birth.

And, as always when he surveyed his inheritance, he thought of his father and of Rhys Lewis ap Siôn Gruffydd, his grandfather. He could trace his ancestry with as much certainty as any gentleman in the neighbourhood—back to Siôn Gruffydd, Nannau, and Hywel ap Siencyn, Ynysmaengwyn, in the time of Elizabeth— even as far back as Sir Roger Kynaston; and on his mother's side to Humphrey, Duke of Gloucester, son of Henry IV. On his father's side he could boast that his lineage went back to Meurig, Lord of Dyfed.

It was strange to think that English blood flowed through his veins, and yet not so strange, since so many of the Welsh had flocked to England during the past hundred and fifty years. At school in Shrewsbury he had felt different from the other boys and he remembered how Dr. Harlow, the history master, had teased him:

'Captain Fluellen, I peeseech you now, will you vouchsafe me, look you, a few disputations with you?' And, naively, he had not understood why the others had laughed. But after a year of learning English, Roman and Greek history, he had come to understand only too well, and this had been the beginning of the conflict between the Welsh and English within him, a conflict which was to last until the end of his days.

Shrewsbury schooldays were a long way behind now. His education had been suddenly interrupted by the death of his father. He had returned to Brynmawr, a boy of seventeen, his appetite for learning whetted but not satisfied. Now he enjoyed teaching Ellis Puw to read. The boy was an avid pupil who gave no trouble, and to be able to share his knowledge and watch Ellis's mind expand and mature gave him intense pleasure.

But the wood for the clogmaker was the pressing task of the moment. Cupping his hands to his mouth he shouted: 'Holo! Ellis!' the call echoing across the fields. Before long he saw the boy running towards him.

Ellis welcomed the chance of going into the town. For one thing he would be free for an hour or two from Huw Morris's incessant teasing. Ever since he had discovered that the young master was teaching the new servant to read there had been no end to it. Huw himself had little taste for learning. Life was too short and there were better things to do. He was not unwilling to describe in detail what some of those things were and enjoyed watching the innocent Ellis blush to the roots of his red hair. Far better for him if he learnt how to fondle Nans y Goetre than those everlasting books, Huw would say, laughing uncontrollably at his own wit.

But Ellis had another reason for wanting to go to Dolgellau that morning. In the iron chest at the foot of his bed there lay a piece of red cloth, knotted at both ends. Ellis was afraid that Huw might see what it contained, especially as there was no key to the chest. He picked up the bundle carefully and placed it on the bed. Then he shut the chest quietly, perhaps too quietly. He was about to take up his bundle again when he heard Huw Morris's voice behind him.

'Why are 'ee playing fox today, Ellis Puw? Have'ee stolen some more books?'

Huw's hulking form filled the doorway. Like most heavy men he could move very quietly and it amused him to follow people, give a sudden shout and then startle his unsuspecting victim. At other times it suited Huw's purpose better to remain silent . . .

By now Ellis was beginning to learn how to handle him. He knew that if he attempted to hide the bundle his secret would be out. Trying to be as natural and as calm as possible, he sat down on the bed, the bundle between his knees.

'The master wants me to take alder wood to the clogmaker in town.'

'What hast 'ee got in that bundle?'

'Oh, this?' said Ellis, raising the bundle carelessly in his hand, his heart beating faster. 'A bit of bread and cheese left over from this morning. Something to munch on my way to town.'

But Huw had lost interest.

'Be'ee going to the Plygain with the men from Brynrhug tonight? Jaist i! I'm looking forward to meeting the boys at the Carw. Parri has promised a jug of hot mead free all round at eleven o'clock before we go on to church with our candles. Be'ee going?'

Huw was more friendly than he had ever been before.

'I'm not going to the Plygain, Huw Morris.'

'The devil take 'ee, what next? Everyone goes to the Plygain at Christmas, even old bookworms like thyself. Too shy or what?'

'No, of course not.'

'Well, 'ee be unnatural then—and un-Christian.'

He wrinkled his forehead suddenly and his eyes became small and watchful. Drawing closer to Ellis he asked slowly, 'Why aren't 'ee going?'

Huw was always amused by Ellis's painful honesty. He could not imagine anyone being stupid enough to be honest if lying made things easier. A curious notion came to him.

Ellis hesitated but his reply when it came was sincere.

'I'm not sure myself why. Something inside me tells me not to go. I can't explain.'

Much to Ellis's surprise Huw did not pursue the matter. Mumbling something about going to the yard, he left the room. Ellis breathed freely and went to load the cart.

It did not take him long to complete his mission to Cadwaladr, the clogmaker. Having delivered the wood, he led the horse and cart away from the Lawnt, past the Church, past Siop Goch and the house of Griffith Tudor the lawyer, and made for Cae Tanws. Since he had hurried on his way to the town, he reckoned he now had about twenty minutes to spare before returning home. Arriving at a stark, ugly building at the furthermost end of the street beside the river Aran, he tied his horse to a nearby post and, with his red bundle held carefully in one hand, he knocked at the door of Cae Tanws jail. After a long delay the warder opened up for him. He was a tall, gaunt man with features as sharp as an eagle's.

'Oh, it's thee again,' was the sour greeting. He knew from experience that he could not expect much of a bribe from this young visitor.

'Yes, Siôn Prys. How is he today?'

'How is *he*? What do you mean? Who is *he*? Hey, d'ye know how many I've got in this jail? Thirty. Thirty wicked scoundrels who pay respect to neither King nor law. How d'ye expect me to know who your *he* is?'

Ellis answered quietly, 'Ifan Roberts, the bailiff of Dolserau. He had a fall last week, do you remember? And broke his leg. How is he?'

Siôn Prys drew a small box from his shirt pocket, took a pinch of snuff between his fingers, held it to his nostrils and breathed in deeply and slowly. Then he asked, 'Have you brought something for him?'

Ellis untied the cloth and showed him the remainder of some bread and cheese and a small blue bowl.

'Something tasty?' asked Siôn Prys, greedily pointing at the bowl.

'Not really.' Ellis took the lid off the bowl and disclosed a yellow, creamy substance. 'Ointment.'

'Ointment!'

'Yes. I made it myself from comfrey leaves. 'Twill heal his leg faster than anything else.'

Surprise and disappointment showed on the face of the warder.

'Ointment,' he repeated, his voice dry with sarcasm, his shoulders shaking with soundless laughter. 'Well, God's blood. Take it to him then. We'll see whether it's your balm or his prayers send him to hell first.'

He held the door wide open and Ellis's nostrils were filled with the smell of cold, damp air. Along a few yards of narrow corridor, they came to the top of some old stone steps. At the bottom of the steps was a door with iron bars across it. Ellis had been to this part of the jail before and, as always, it made him want to vomit. Only those who gave money or other offerings to Siôn Prys and brought food for the prisoners were permitted to see their friends and relatives, and since these creatures relied for sustenance on what their visitors brought with them, Ellis knew what to expect as soon as that door was opened.

First, hope would light up in the lifeless eyes of the prisoners — then disappointment. There would follow tears, entreaties, swearing and cursing.

How he pitied these poor people, some of them there for having stolen a sheep or a horse, who knew that execution awaited them.

Others had fallen into debt. One girl, a half-wit, was to be hanged because she had drowned her child.

Ellis had almost forgotten how bad the stench was. The only light came from a hole high in the wall, near the ceiling, and the strong iron bars across it put an end to any thought of escape. A cold wind blew cruelly through this opening but even that was not enough to purify the air.

The prisoners stood up to their ankles in a strongly smelling miasma — a mixture of rain, soil and human excrement. Small mounds of straw lay here and there, seized by the lucky few, who had fought viciously for them.

Ellis peered anxiously through the huge bars that separated himself and the warder from the prisoners, but he could not see his friend. Siôn Prys walked on, ignoring the prisoners' shouts and groans, until he came to another cell, hardly more than a closet. But it was clean and quiet, with plenty of fresh straw on the floor.

'Your friend has a comfortable bed to lie on,' grumbled the warder, unlocking a square door set into the bars. 'The Quakers are fortunate in their rich friends.'

Ifan Robarts lay with his face to the wall, but he tried to move when he heard the warder's voice. Ellis was distressed to see the deterioration in Ifan's appearance since his last visit.

He had been a strong man, a happy, healthy man. Surely this was not Ifan, the man who turned dark, pleading eyes towards him, beads of sweat glistening on his forehead?

Ellis rushed into the room and the shadow of a smile crossed Ifan's face, making it more familiar.

He spoke with difficulty, 'It's good to see thee, Friend.'

'Are 'ee worse, Ifan Robarts? It's that leg, is it?'

But the effort of speaking had caused Ifan's eyes to close again. Ellis knelt beside the sick man and gently but deftly tore off the rags that had once been breeches. He drew in his breath sharply. The leg had swollen to twice its normal size and was badly discoloured. From the flesh a piece of bone jutted out like a branch half-torn from a tree. Ellis turned furiously to the warder.

'Hasn't anyone seen to this leg?'

'Seen to the leg? What the devil d'ye think I am? An apothe-cary?'

'Ifan Robarts broke his leg trying to separate two men who were about to kill each other—in fact, he was trying to keep order in thy jail, Siôn Prys.'

Ellis spoke quietly so as not to upset Ifan but Siôn Prys rounded on him.

'Look here, ye shameless jackanapes. Don't ye know that it's a heretic and a blasphemer who lies there? If God has struck him down I'll be damned if I'm going to play nursemaid to him.'

Ifan opened his eyes slowly. 'Never mind, Ellis. Thou hast come and I'm glad to see thee.'

Turning his back on the warder who had lumbered away angrily, Ellis opened the box of ointment.

'Don't talk now, Ifan. Here is some comfrey balsam to put on thy leg. But first I must try and put that bone back—can 'ee bear it? The master said I worked a miracle on a young calf back home a month ago—slowly now—there we are—I'll pull that leg down ... like this ... '

While Ellis spoke quietly with the tenderness of a mother for her child, his fingers were busy. For one so frail his hands were nimble and strong. He would have liked to have asked Siôn Prys for water to wash the wound but he was afraid to leave Ifan in case he would not be permitted to return.

The sick man's body trembled as with an ague but not a sigh came from his lips. Ellis looked around for cloth to bandage the leg but there was none. Then he remembered the red bundle. At least the cloth was made of pure wool. He tore it into strips and tied them tightly round Ifan's leg from knee to ankle. The ointment seeped into the wound and at once Ifan felt some relief from pain.

'Thou would'st make a good doctor,' he said, in a voice already stronger.

Ellis looked about him. 'This is a better room than the other. How did 'ee manage to get here?'

Ifan's eyes lit up. 'Robert Owen, Dolserau, came to see me. He's just been released. He gave Siôn Prys a tidy bit of money to have me moved here. I didn't want special treatment but the master said I'd get well sooner on my own and in any case it was almost time for me to be free.'

'How long hast 'ee been here now, Ifan?'

'I don't know, it's hard to remember. February, I think . . . but what does it matter? Hast thou seen Sinai lately?'

Ellis smiled. 'Yes, I was over there last night. She's all right but pining for thee.'

'And the children?'

'As lively and as full of mischief as thou would'st have them be. Ellyw keeps chattering away and she's almost walking now.'

'Is she? What does she say?'

Ellis repeated some of the funny sayings of the youngest of the nine little ones, who were already beginning to forget their father's face. He did not mention Steffan's cough nor that Lisa had been missing for three days. Poor Sinai. It was hard enough for any wife to be left to look after nine children on her own. But for her it was harder: she depended so much on her husband at every turn. Without him she was like a bird without its mate, and Ellis admired her courage all the more because she was so aware of her own shortcomings.

'I don't understand Ifan's ideas, Ellis,' she had told him. 'But I know he's a good man and one of God's children. And I know that whatever happens he has right on his side. Don't tell him about Steffan, will 'ee?' she had begged, as she stroked the limp locks of the child lying on the dishevelled bed.

Ifan had closed his eyes again and Ellis smiled at him.

'Are 'ee sleeping, Ifan? Don't until I've told 'ee some good news. Are 'ee listening?'

Ifan opened his eyes with an effort but summoned up a smile.

'Thee won't be here long, Ifan Robarts. 'Tis rumoured that the King will pardon all those who are in prison for matters of conscience. Many have already been released and Robert Owen, Dolserau, is doing his very best for 'ee at this moment.'

Ifan had turned his face to the shadows and it was difficult for Ellis to see how this had affected him. Then, the quiet voice said, 'That is good . . . How's the reading coming on, Ellis?'

The boy smiled. 'Very well. I have no difficulty now.'

28

'And Rowland Ellis, is he drawing nearer to us?'

'I don't know. It's hard to know what is in the master's mind. I sometimes think he is longing to join us but isn't able to take the first step.'

'He'll come in God's good time. Did 'ee get any more books from Jane Owen?'

'She says I've read almost everything that's been printed in Welsh. She suggested I might learn English so as to be able to read the works of the blind poet Milton and some of the religious books. But somehow I'm not very concerned. I think I shall have little need of the English tongue. I would most like to be able to read the works of our own poets. They say that old Robert Vaughan left a big collection of them at Hengwrt. I've heard too that the verses of the Vicar of Llandovery have just been published. I'd like . . .'

He looked at Ifan but it seemed as if he were asleep. Ellis thought he had better leave and return when there was another excuse to come to the town. He got up quietly and went towards the door but stopped short as he heard Ifan whispering excitedly. He had raised himself to a half-sitting position and his face was deathly pale. His eyes were staring and he grasped the straw on his bed tightly till his knuckles shone white with the effort.

'Ellis, thou must listen. I saw him . . . George Fox . . . in the town with John ap John . . . no, don't go . . . stay and hear what I have to say.'

His voice was low but clear. ' "The true Light which is given to every man who is born". That's what he said. "The only divine light which enables men . . . to understand His words and to recognise their sins." Ellis, tell Sinai . . .'

But fever robbed the rest of his words of all meaning. Ellis did not know what to do. He was already late and he had done all he could to make Ifan comfortable. He dared not ask Siôn Prys to call a doctor. He knew what answer he would receive. Perhaps the fever would die down before long. He took a last look at Ifan's unfamiliar face, then turned and left the room.

3

For the first time since Ann's birth Meg was venturing out alone on horseback. Usually, when she wished to go into the town, she would ride behind her husband; but not tonight, for the blue velvet dress under the merino wool cloak was far too voluminous for her to share his saddle in comfort.

She was an expert horse woman, and rode side saddle with her back as straight as a queen's. The animal warmth that came from Barnabas always pleased her and she was glad that the path from Bryn Mawr to the town was too rough for a carriage.

Frost shone on the trees and fields and only the clip-clop of the horse's hooves broke the silence. Meg gazed contentedly at the tall figure of Rowland riding in front of her. She would not be ashamed of him at Hengwrt. He was as handsome as any man in the neighbourhood. Would he join in the dancing before the Plygain? She hoped so, but it was hard to tell with him these days. How solemn he had become. Hywel Vaughan—now there was an interesting man. He must be nearing fifty but how attractive he was with his black periwig and fine clothes. She loved to hear him talk about the Court in London, although sometimes his stories made her blush. Lord, how glad she was to be able to enjoy herself once again! Glad, of course, that she had a child, but, heigho, glad, too, that she had old Malan to take care of it. She was too young, too beautiful to lock herself away in the mountains—not her words but Hywel Vaughan's. She had not repeated them to Rowland, for he would surely have misunderstood. A gentle pleasantry called for a light retort. There was challenge and a hint of danger in playing this little game of double meaning with a man as quick-witted as Hywel Vaughan. Somehow she did not think Rowland would approve.

The town was lively. People hurried hither and thither, noses red and eyes bright with the cold. Snow would fall before morning, they told each other, hearing the moaning of the wind. And many recalled the ice-bound winter of six years before. What a winter that had been. For the first time in history the River Wnion had been a solid block of ice from one end to the other. Rumour had it that the River Thames in London had frozen so hard that they had been able to sell roast chestnuts to the skaters from stalls on the ice. In the parishes of Talybont and Penllyn old people and the very young froze to death, and foxes came down to the town from Cader Idris in search of food. Pray God to preserve them from such another winter!

Men rushed into the taverns to warm themselves with ale and mead. Women scuttled from one house to the other preparing for the *cymortha* at Plasgwyn for Guto Pandy's widow. Barnabas and Ned trotted through the crowds and the master and mistress of Bryn Mawr were soon over the bridge on their way to Hengwrt.

Brilliant lights greeted them from chandeliers in the hall at Hengwrt, and a man in sumptuous livery opened the great doors to them. At the foot of the wide oak staircase Hywel Vaughan and his wife Lowri stood to receive their guests. Meg caught her breath at the splendour before her.

Hywel was dressed in scarlet with white ruffles at his neck and wrists. A white waistcoat with gold buttons fitted his body tightly and green ribbons secured the frills of his trousers. His finely-curled periwig fell over his shoulders. Compared with his elegance, Meg noted with a hint of malice, Lowri Vaughan's grey gown was plain and drab. A brown fichu robbed her long, pinched face of all colour and emphasised rather than disguised the flatness of her breasts.

Sounds of merriment came from the dining hall. In an alcove above the staircase a small orchestra of five musicians had started to play for the dancers, and Meg felt the familiar thrill that set her feet a-tapping.

'Rowland and Meg, my kinsmen, so you have arrived! Welcome to Hengwrt, lady . . . and welcome back to life.' Hywel Vaughan bowed low as though sweeping the floor with an imaginary hat. Lowri smiled sourly at them, then turned to welcome Colonel Price, Rhiwlas, and his wife. That puts us in our place, Meg told herself, storing the incident in her memory. One day she would repay Lowri Vaughan. In the meantime she smiled sweetly at the master of the house and curtsied before moving on to the room set aside for the ladies. Rowland was waiting for her when she returned and Meg felt a twinge of annoyance as she noticed his unsmiling face.

'Try at least to look as though you are enjoying yourself,' she whispered peevishly, and realised that Lowri Vaughan's snub must have penetrated deeply to put her out so. But before long Lowri, and Rowland too, were forgotten. The orchestra had struck up a new French dance, the *Bourrée*, and Hywel Vaughan was partnering her for the first dance. She held her head high, trying to ignore the beating of her heart. She was born to be a lady and live in a mansion. Her grace and dignity were more suited to Hengwrt than Lowri's boorish manners. The music, the bright lights and the merriment were as heady as wine. She knew that people were watching her and this knowledge was as sweet as honey. She threw back her head confidently.

'Tell me, cousin, what is the latest news from London?'

'Well, now, the Declaration of Indulgence has been passed. The war against the Low Countries goes from bad to worse . . . '

He was teasing her. He knew well what was in her mind. 'No, not politics — I've little interest. The Court, the King . . . who is the latest?'

Hywel Vaughan laughed aloud. 'If you came to London, mistress, they would all have to be on their mettle. Remember this, 'twas a Welshwoman was one of the first.'

Meg blushed but was in her element. 'Lucy Walters, wasn't it?'

'Yes, but she's gone into oblivion long ago. Mistress Palmer has just been created a Duchess. But, of course, the chief favourite is Nelly.'

'Nelly?'

'Yes, Nell Gwyn.'

'Another Welshwoman?'

'Perhaps indeed. No one knows exactly where she sprung from. She used to sell oranges in Drury Lane. Then she became an actress.'

'An actress!'

'Don't be alarmed. She was good. And there's not much shame attached to being an actress these days, believe me. But Nell need worry about acting no longer. The King has promised her son a dukedom and you may be sure she herself hardly goes short of the best things in life.'

'Oh, I'd love to go to London,' sighed Meg.

'To be the King's mistress?' asked Hywel, smiling. And they both laughed as though sharing a secret.

Rowland stood by one of the pillars watching them. He knew that the bouts of depression that overcame him these days were likely to alienate Meg. A year or two ago Rowland Ellis would have been among the merriest of the company, but things, or he himself, had changed. For some reason he thought of Ellis Puw and felt at that moment closer to his servant with his fustian breeches and rough woollen shirt than to this present company in their brightly-coloured silks and satins. How much did he really know about these people? He knew how many sheep Richard Nannau, Cefndeuddwr, owned; how many servants Robert Fychan, Caerynwch, employed. But did he know anything of importance about them? Such as—well, what? What is it important to know about a man? Has he self-knowledge? Are there within him islands of loneliness and uncertainty? Is he afraid of old age and death? Does he long for wealth, fame, love?

A gawky woman brushed past him on her way to the ballroom from the dining hall where she had obviously stayed too long with the wine. Her partner, a prosperous farmer from Bala way, lumbered up behind her, red-faced and bleary-eyed. Where was man's dignity to be found today? Not in these surroundings, in spite of their splendour. In the Church with all its holy ceremony? Later on the guests would be walking in procession towards the church, each one carrying a candle, singing praises to a babe born in a stable. The noise and merriment would reach their height. Well, what was wrong with that? The coming of the Lord was a joyous happening. Why should not king and commoner alike celebrate it with gaiety?

Suddenly Betsan's face appeared before his eyes, her yellow

wrinkles dripping with water from the River Wnion, her heavy eyelids closed against the hatred, the shame and mockery that surrounded her. Since the day he had been a reluctant witness to Betsan's drowning, the old woman had thrust herself into his consciousness, particularly at those times when he wanted to believe that all was in God's hands. The drowning of witches was no uncommon event; indeed, during Archbishop Laud's time it had been considered the solemn duty of responsible and good Christians. More than one had been ducked in the Red Chair during the past year and had not come out of the ordeal alive. So why should he be so concerned about Betsan? Every time she entered his mind, her face and old body became more and more ugly until the very thought of her had become a nightmare. And always he would try to turn his thoughts from her to the most beautiful thing he knew, his own wife. But the two would dissolve into each other, and by now he knew that Betsan was Meg and Meg was Betsan.

He choked at the thought. His eyes scanned the dancers, searching for his wife but she was nowhere among them. The pace of the dancing had increased. Overhead one of the chandeliers was swaying slowly, but he was the only one who noticed. A man threw his partner's silk shawl up in the air and a shriek of laughter rose from the rest of the group as they watched it descend slowly towards the floor.

Where was Meg? The Bala farmer's periwig sat awry on his head while his wife—if, indeed, she was his wife—doubled up with laughter. The orchestra was no longer playing a *Bourrée* or Minuet but had launched into a rollicking country dance, *Pwt ar y Bys*. All the dancers let themselves go and pranced backwards and forwards, carefully arranged hair falling down, coat tails flying this way and that.

In a corner of the room, behind one of the pillars, a small knot of men had turned their backs on the dancers and were concentrating on the black and white dice being thrown on the table by each in turn. Money rapidly changed hands and the solemnity of this group contrasted oddly with the ribald gaiety of the rest of the room.

He must find Meg. What if she were ill? After all, it was not long since the birth of Ann. Where on earth could she have gone? Pushing his way towards a door at the far end of the room, he hesitated a moment before opening it, but by now anxiety filled his mind. He was not willing to admit why he hesitated but it had not escaped his notice that Hywel Vaughan had also been missing from the company.

Slowly he opened the door. Then, trying to make his voice sound natural, he called out 'Meg?' But there was no reply. Candles burned at either end of the room and in their light Rowland saw that the walls were lined with books—hundreds of them. This must have been old Robert Vaughan's library. He leaned his back against the door and surrendered himself to the welcome peace of the room. He was grateful at that moment for the silent companionship of books, a refuge from the raucous company on the other side of the door.

But he was not alone in the room. Someone rose from the oak window-seat hidden in the shadows. For a moment he did not realise who it was. He was conscious of a graceful middle-aged woman, but when he did recognise her, he was surprised at her presence in that house.

He had not seen Jane Owen, Hywel Vaughan's sister, for some years, but, like everyone else in the neighbourhood, he had heard rumours about her and her husband. Robert Owen, Dolserau, had been imprisoned several times. The Quakers were mostly people one could laugh at, but after the passing of the Conventicle Act they had also been feared. Some thought they were secret Papists working for the restoration of the old faith. Others said they were plotting against Parliament, seeking to destroy all that had been gained at such high cost during the Civil War. And because everyone was so anxious to prove his allegiance to the Church and to the Government, knowing the penalties for even suspected defection, each vied with the other in proclaiming his hatred of the Quakers.

It was surprising that so many had clung for so long to this peculiar creed, which forbade men to take off their hats indoors and where everyone, whatever his status, was addressed by the familiar 'thee' and 'thou'. Following that early fervour created by George Fox—'the man in leather breeches'—on his visit to the town fifteen years earlier, many had joined the sect, and neither humiliation nor imprisonment had so far weakened their spirit.

A man's social status had little to do with it. Weaver, cobbler, turner, cooper, all had joined the sect, but most of them were farmers, small landowners and their servants. Nevertheless, it had amazed the people of Dolgellau that Robert Owen should have been drawn to their ranks. A descendant of Baron Owen, murdered by the Red Bandits a century before, here was a man who had been an ardent Parliamentarian and Puritan during the Civil War, and, as Justice of the Peace, had been known to act severely towards the King's supporters. Maesygarnedd had implied that this severity had driven men to hypocrisy, forcing them to profess an allegiance to Parliament which was insincere. He had been feared throughout the county. What wonder then that people feared the Quakers as well? Had not Robert Owen's name been associated with the Fifth Monarchists? And had he not collected money throughout the country for General Harrison's army? Indeed, it was on account of this that he had spent fifteen weeks in Bala jail.

No one knew exactly what had happened to him there. But when Robert Owen left the jail he had become a different man. Whereas he had once been hectoring and intemperate of speech he was now gentle and compassionate. It was well known that there were Quaker meetings at Dolserau and the authorities would have been glad to lay their hands on him once again. But curiously enough he remained unmolested. Some said it was because he was the brother-in-law of Hywel Vaughan, the high sheriff of the county. So Ifan Robarts, his bailiff, had been jailed in his stead— for not attending the parish church.

If family pride had saved the high sheriff's brother-in-law from jail, there was no doubt whatsoever about Hywel's personal feelings towards Robert. It had been difficult enough for Hywel to achieve his ambition of becoming high sheriff and if those in authority had known of the activities of some of his family his present power would have been far less. He did his best to see that the gap between him and the Dolserau family was as wide as possible. Small wonder then that Rowland was surprised to find Jane Owen in her old home that night.

'I beg your pardon, Mistress Owen. I did not know—'

Jane Owen said quietly, 'Rowland Ellis, isn't it? I'm pleased to see thee.'

The use of the familiar pronoun struck Rowland strangely. He hesitated to use it even to his servants, and he certainly did not know Jane Owen well enough to warrant her using it to him. That was another thing about the Quakers that irritated him and he answered her curtly.

'I am looking for my wife. She is not here I see.'

'Don't go on my account, Rowland Ellis. It's peaceful here.'

Rowland realised how weary he was. Somewhere a clock chimed ten. It would be another hour before the company started for the Plygain.

'This was my father's library,' said Jane Owen, her gentle eyes moving round the room. 'I've not been here for six years— not since his death. Thou art surely too young to remember him?'

'I remember him,' said Rowland. 'I was sixteen when he died.'

He recalled how the hoodlums of the town would run after the old antiquarian teasing him for his absentminded manner. There had always been a distant look in his eyes, a look which did not belong to the turbulence of the century. Aneirin, Taliesin and the ancient Princes—they were his companions. There was the same dream-like look in his daughter's eyes. She was between fifty and sixty. Her grey hair was coiled across the crown of her head, with none of the frivolous curls and fringes that adorned the heads of most women of her rank. What impressed Rowland most was her serenity. Jane Owen must have suffered greatly when her husband was in jail and she herself shunned by her family. One would expect this suffering to show on her face. Certainly there were deep furrows above her eyebrows and her neck was too thin. But there was no trace of bitterness and disappointment. Just as the father's face had seemed to belong to another world, so, too, did the daughter's, except that Robert Vaughan's world was of the past whereas Jane Owen's was of the spirit.

'Ellis Puw has told me about thee.'

37

'Has he? You know Ellis?'

She smiled. 'Thou hast taught him to read so well he has run through all my Welsh books.'

This was news to Rowland. 'So it was you. I had no idea who was lending him books.'

'No, Ellis believes in the old saying, "Wise is the silent man". He was afraid of thy displeasure.'

Rowland's eyes widened. 'Displeasure? Why should I show displeasure?'

'But dost thou not know we are a dangerous family? Ellis was afraid his master would forbid him to visit us.'

'But that's—'

'Unreasonable? Yes, but it has happened before to others. And Ellis has such regard for Rowland Ellis that it would break his heart to have to leave his service.'

Rowland looked at her, his eyes sharp.

'If there's such danger of Rowland Ellis behaving in this way why has Jane Owen revealed his servant's secret?'

There was a moment's hesitation before the quiet response.

'Because Jane Owen suspects that Rowland Ellis has already experienced for himself the strength of the Inner Light.'

The words stung Rowland. He struggled to deny their implication. His future was comfortably established: Bryn Mawr, his life as a small squire of honourable descent, his books and all that he had learnt at his school in Shrewsbury to enrich his leisure, the respect of his friends—and Meg. He was reluctant to admit that it was she who had woven the pattern of his life for him. His own desires were nothing. They were like clay in the hands of a potter. He knew with certainty that if he deviated in the slightest from this pattern Meg would be lost to him for ever. The significance of Jane Owen's words, added to his present concern for Meg, were more than he could bear.

'I've no idea what makes you think you can read my thoughts so well,' he said coldly. At the same time he was ashamed of being so childish. But he would admit nothing to this strange woman, who stood before him so serene and self-assured. He tried to think of an excuse to change the subject or to take his leave gracefully, but she forestalled him.

'The Friends will be meeting at Dolserau on New Year's Eve. Thou art very welcome to join us.'

Rowland had no chance to reply. Someone was pushing the door open clumsily with much noise and laughter. A man's voice mingled with a woman's half-protesting.

'In here . . . only for a moment . . . '

Hywel Vaughan's speech was thick but the meaning of the urgency in his voice was clear enough. He drew Meg into the library and Rowland's heart sank as he realised why her eyes looked so strange and her lips so slack. The blue velvet dress had slipped from one shoulder and she made no attempt to adjust it.

Silence froze the room as the two slowly realised they were not alone. Meg began to laugh nervously. Hywel tried at once to conceal the situation by shouting with unnatural heartiness.

'Well, Rowland, you old rascal, hiding yourself away here.'

He stopped abruptly and the grin vanished as he realised that his sister was there too. Rowland sensed that a new feeling pervaded the room—a stony hatred. What passed from brother to sister was almost palpable.

'And what may you be doing here?'

The Hywel Vaughan who now confronted them was a stranger to Rowland Ellis—and to Meg. The debonair confidence of the man of the world had vanished. No hint now in the harsh voice of the gallantry and good breeding that had captivated Meg. She, like Rowland, was stunned by his savage look and harsh words.

Rowland scarcely dared look at Jane Owen, but when he did he marvelled at her composure. She remained silent as she regarded her brother.

'Answer me, you hussy. What are you doing here? You know well enough I'll not have you at Hengwrt.'.

'I've not come here tonight on my own behalf, Hywel, but to beg a favour of thee—on Christmas Eve.'

Hywel began to curse her for her temerity but she interrupted him.

'If Christmas means anything to thee, Hywel, if the birth of the

Prince of Peace has any meaning at all for thee, thou must listen to me tonight. I'll not come here again, I promise. But if thou dost feel any mercy tonight I beg thee spare a little for our bailiff, Ifan Robarts.'

Hywel looked as if he were going to choke.

'My God, your bailiff! I keep your husband out of jail, where he belongs, for the sake of our good name And now you expect me to do likewise for your servant.'

'A man's position has nothing to do with it. Thou knowst very well that the Declaration of Indulgence is law. Why then is Ifan Roberts still in jail? He never harmed a soul and he has committed no crime. He's dying, Hywel. Dost 'ee hear? The power to free him is thine—and 'tis thy duty. He will have to be released sooner or later, but it's urgent now, Hywel. Ifan needs his wife's care. Let him go to her for pity's sake.'

Hywel's reply was to open the door for his sister.

'Hywel, he has nine little children.'

'I care not if he has a hundred. I am the one to decide whether or not a man should be set free and I need no advice from law-breakers like you and your husband. Did you for one moment think that I would listen to you of all people?'

'No, I did not,' replied Jane Owen, dispiritedly.

'I am waiting for you to go. I have guests here tonight.' Hywel emphasised the word 'guests'.

Jane Owen walked slowly towards the door, and as she passed her brother said with an irony he could not ignore: 'I hope I've not made thee late for the Plygain.' Then, turning to Rowland, she added, 'God be with thee, Rowland Ellis. Perhaps my visit has not been in vain after all.'

There was an uncomfortable silence when she had gone. Hywel Vaughan was the first to regain his composure, and, reluctantly, Rowland had to admire his self control. The smooth demeanour of the man-of-the-world returned, as though nothing untoward had happened.

'My apologies for that disturbance,' he said lightly, as if apologising for a servant who had dropped a dish. He brushed an imaginary spot from his sleeve and adjusted the ruffle at his neck.

'Well, we'd better assemble the rest of the party and make for the church.' But Rowland noticed that his breathing was heavy and an angry colour still showed on his neck.

Suddenly, Meg burst into tears. The events of the night had been too much for her and she wept with relief at the return of the Hywel she knew in place of the stranger. But for the first time Rowland realised that he loathed his cousin and his loathing was more for the mask that Hywel presented to the world than for the cold cruelty of the real man. He asked himself whether he felt this way because of Meg or because of Hywel's behaviour towards his sister. With surprise he decided that it was the latter—at that moment, at least. He could therefore move towards his wife and put his arm around her. With a sigh Meg laid her head against his shoulder and began to sob. Rowland turned to Hywel and said calmly:

'With your permission, cousin, we will not come to the Plygain tonight, after all. As you see, Meg is worn out. It is better that we retire.'

Hywel was full of sympathy—and relief, thought Rowland, his dislike giving edge to his understanding.

'Of course . . . of course. I'm sorry, mistress, that you should have been upset by my sister like this. I hope you will be able to forget the unfortunate encounter.'

Rowland remembered in time that Hywel Vaughan was his host and that while under his cousin's roof he must not give the reply that came readily to his lips. 'It was not your sister who upset Meg.'

'Come, Meg,' he murmured as if she were a little child and led her up the wide staircase to the room that had been prepared for them. Before entering the bedroom, he looked down from the gallery and saw Hywel at the door of the hall calling for silence, bidding the servants bring a candle for each of the guests to carry in the procession to the Church. Rowland gave a low sigh. He was grateful for the excuse, however unpleasant, not to have to witness the same spectacle as last year, when sixty drunken people had made their way towards the Church after the celebrations at Hengwrt. They had been joined by the townspeople who were

41

hardly in better state. It was a wonder the Church had not been burnt to the ground since even small children, half asleep, carried candles. But children were better trusted with candles than some of the older ones. For that night the bellringer had slipped and fallen across the threshold of the church and broken his leg, and Kit Thomas's baby had died through being given too much ale by its mother. And judging by the company at Hengwrt, similar misadventures might well occur again.

He shut the door quietly behind him. Meg was slumped across the bed. How black her hair was against the white coverlet and how limp now was the splendid new gown. Rowland could not see her face for one arm was hiding it. A strange new emotion came over him. He felt old, old, old, not physically but in experience and understanding. Meg was just a child to him. He gazed at his wife with profound love—and peace.

'Meg—' he began. But there was no response. He stroked her hair but she did not stir.

'Meg—my love—'

She murmured something unintelligible.

'Come. Let me help you.'

Like a mother with her child, Rowland turned his wife gently on to her back and started to undo the small gilt buttons of her gown. The dancing flames of the fire threw strange shadows on the whiteness of her body. Rowland drew the curtains around the bed before climbing in beside his wife, and snuffing out the candles.

4

The news of Ifan Robarts's death reached Ellis Puw in the town three days after Christmas.

At once he rushed up to Brithdir to see Sinai, feeling desperately sorry for her and her nine children. He opened the door of the cottage slowly and called her name. The sound of a child crying in the darkness reached his ears, and the voice of a girl, not much more than a child herself, consoling it. At least Dorcas was there. Where were the other children? He called out gently to the eldest daughter of Sinai and Ifan, but it was Sinai who replied.

When his eyes had become accustomed to the darkness, he saw the widow sitting in a chair by the fireplace—but there was no fire in it. Dorcas had a light in the bedroom, probably Sinai's only candle, thought Ellis.

'Come in, Ellis Puw.'

The baby, Ellyw, was asleep in her mother's arms but Ellis could have sworn that Sinai was not aware that she was nursing it. She held the untidy bundle loosely on her knee and if the little one had fallen to the ground Sinai would barely have noticed. She sat like a statue, her hair straggling untidily over her shoulders. Steffan started to cough again, which at least put a stop to his crying. Dorcas was murmuring, 'There, there, love. Tha'll be well soon.'

'Sinai, there's no fire. Let me light one.'

'Isn't there?' Sinai turned her head slightly and shivered, as if aware for the first time of the cold. 'Oh, thank 'ee, Ellis.'

Ellis went to look for wood and peat. He did not bother to ask Sinai where they were stored. She would not have known at the best of times. Before long, the flames were blazing and a smell of damp wood burning sweetly filled the shabby room.

'What about food? When did you last eat?'

Sinai shook her head. 'I haven't much appetite. But Dorcas . . . I'm sure she would . . . '

Ellis crossed to the bedroom. A child of about six lay flat on his back, his little body as thin and feeble as a wren's in the rain. His sister knelt at his side, gently pressing a damp cloth to his feverish brow. Ellis could see great dark circles under the boy's eyes and a face as white as chalk. The girl, Dorcas, was fifteen but looked thirty.

'Dorcas,' he whispered, 'I'll take over for a while. You go and get something to eat.'

The girl looked at him gratefully and got up. The smell of sickness filled the air as he took her place. It was a pity people had not realised how important windows were when they built houses, he thought. People suffering from consumption ought to have plenty of fresh air and daylight. There was only one window in the whole cottage, a small one on the outer wall of what was called 'the hall'. He looked down at the child and thought what little hope he had of reaching boyhood let alone manhood. Another bout of coughing wracked the emaciated body. Very gently Ellis turned him on one side, placing his hand on the boy's forehead. Suddenly the coughing ceased and the little boy gave a long sigh. Ellis stroked the wan cheek and was gratified to see that Steffan was breathing naturally and deeply. Before long he was fast asleep.

'What did 'ee do to him, Ellis?'

Sinai was standing at his side, looking down at Steffan, as though she could hardly believe her eyes. Ellis made a sign to her not to make a sound and led her back to the chair by the fire. Sinai looked as though she had witnessed a miracle. For the first time hope came back into her eyes.

'Dost 'ee think he will live, Ellis Puw?'

Ellis hardly knew how to answer. They both had seen dozens of children dying from the same illness as Steffan's. But Sinai clung to this new hope as if to an anchor. Perhaps this was a sign from God. She had not seen Steffan sleep so soundly since Ifan went away. But Ellis was afraid of giving her too much hope.

'If the Lord wishes him to go to his father, Sinai Robarts, we must do all we can to let him go peacefully.'

As soon as he had spoken he was sorry because the words sounded cold and cruel. But Sinai looked straight at him, not flinching.

'If it be God's will,' she said.

Dorcas was at the fireside heating the broth and, observing the quiet way she moved around the room preparing the meal, Ellis thought, if one in the family is untidy, another must make up for it.

Dorcas had learnt this lesson early. Her cap and apron were as white as could be after being whisked in a crock full of water from the river, then squeezed with a wooden roller. Ellis knew of her skill with the spinning wheel and indeed all the children, apart from the youngest, had their allotted task—picking the wool from the hedges, spinning and carding, gathering herbs for the weaver to dye the cloth. There would be even more need now of everyone's help.

He enquired after the other children. Sinai pointed towards the loft where two of the youngest were sleeping, explaining that Jane Owen had taken the other five to Dolserau, to give her time to recover a little.

'She wanted us all to go there, but I couldn't think of leaving here—not yet at any rate.'

'What will 'ee do now, Sinai Robarts?' asked Ellis anxiously, after a few minutes' silence.

Sinai's reply was unexpectedly definite.

'I shall do what hundreds have done before me,' she said. 'Perhaps Dorcas and Lisa can go into service and Sioned will be ten in February. There may be a place for her somewhere. 'Tis a pity the boys are so young. Except Gutyn, of course. He's eleven. Robert Owen has promised him a place at once. And Dafydd can go to him when he's nine. No good thinking of work for Huw and Lowri yet,' she added, with a faint smile, looking towards the loft.

Suddenly Sinai threw her arms around his neck.

'Oh, Ellis, th'art so kind. And so young. How old bist 'ee? Sixteen? But th'art a tower of strength to me. Don't let me become a burden—but promise to come and see Steffan often.'

They barely heard the gentle knock on the door. Sinai was not expecting a visitor at that time of night.

She whispered fearfully to Ellis. 'Who can it be?'

He stepped towards the door and opened it to his master, who showed no surprise at finding Ellis there.

'Is Sinai Robarts in?'

Ellis stood aside for Rowland Ellis to enter and his heart pounded. He knew somehow that this was a fateful moment. His master looked at Sinai and the wretchedness around her, and he was heart-sick at what he saw. But Sinai's fear prevented her from seeing his pity. She held her child tightly to her. Was not the master of Bryn Mawr a friend of Hywel Vaughan? Perhaps he was angry at finding Ellis Puw there and perhaps he had come to warn him to stay away in future. If so, she would be better dead.

Rowland sensed her thoughts. He held out his hand.

'I came to say how deeply sorry I am, Sinai Robarts.'

She continued to look at him with uncertainty but it slowly dawned on her that he had come there that night as a friend, not as an enemy. A new hope showed in her eyes and suddenly her hand was in his.

He threw open his black cloak and they saw that he was carrying a bag.

'I hope you will accept these few things—perhaps they will help for a little while.' And he took out a huge cheese, a sack of wheatmeal and some eggs, and placed them on the table.

Tears rolled down Sinai's cheeks. Her frozen anguish melted in the warmth of his kindness. Suddenly she was aware of Ifan's presence in the room and almost turned to say, 'Aren't they kind to us, my love?' And although she knew only too well that Ifan was not in the room, a peace came over her then that was to remain with her to the end of her days.

Rowland began to ask about the children. What arrangements had she made for them? As Ellis listened to the gentle voice questioning Sinai, encouraging her to talk about her problems and offering suggestions, he marvelled at his master's tact and intuition. That is where education tells, he thought, without envy. Rowland's long, curling hair and slender hands under the ruffle of black silk were almost feminine. But there was a strength of leadership in his voice and in his penetrating eyes. His master had been born a gentleman, just as he, Ellis Puw, had been born to be a shepherd.

'We need another maidservant at Bryn Mawr,' declared Rowland. 'Could one of your girls come there?'

Sinai looked at Dorcas. 'Well, sir, I could not wish for anything better. I'm sure—'

But Dorcas had become anxious. 'No, not me, mother,' she whispered urgently. 'Begging your pardon, sir. But who would look after Steffan?'

'Of course,' said her mother vaguely. 'I had forgotten. She has a way with Steffan—much better than mine. I'm sorry, sir, if we seem to be ungrateful. But Lisa will be needing a place. And if she will do . . . well, she's fourteen and very strong . . . '.

Ellis Puw was conscious of a pang of disappointment, though he did not quite know why. Lisa was a good girl but . . . Rowland drew his cloak around him and made for the door.

'Lisa it shall be then. Send her over tomorrow.' He turned to his servant. 'Will you be walking home with me, Ellis Puw?'

Ellis nodded and rushed to open the door for his master. But before he went Sinai's hand caught at his.

'Remember, won't 'ee, Ellis Puw. Come and see Steffan soon. Promise?'

'I promise, Sinai Robarts,' replied Ellis. But he was looking at Dorcas as he spoke.

The two men walked in silence for about half a mile. Before them rose the blackness of Cader Idris like the fist of night itself. Snow had not yet fallen. They had said it would fall on Christmas Eve, but tonight the wind howled mournfully, for the storm was on its way at last. When they reached the meadow known as Tir Stent, Rowland stopped and took a deep breath.

'Isn't the air here wonderful—where mountain and valley winds meet?'

Ellis replied eagerly. 'Strange you should have said that, sir. Do you know what Ifan Robarts told me? That . . .'

He hesitated. Rowland looked at him inquiringly.

'That what?'

Ellis's words came slowly and thoughtfully. 'That someone—an

Englishman—passed this way on his journey down to Dolgellau. And, as he breathed this air, he raised his hands and told his companion that God would raise up a chosen people from this place to set under his teaching.'

Rowland knew the answer already but he asked; 'Who was that man, Ellis?'

There was a moment's pause before Ellis replied.

'George Fox, the Quaker.'

The two men stood silently while the moorland wind wrapped itself around them. They felt free now that they knew they could speak of things that had been a barrier between them for months.

'What else did Ifan Robarts say to you?'

Ellis Puw started to speak, his voice becoming stronger and more confident as he went on.

'Ifan said that the Scriptures had been sent by God to bear witness to simple people about the light. But the Scriptures are not the light. The Apostle said—"Know for yourselves that Jesus Christ is within ye . . ." If the fishermen and unlettered men of old had believed the learned men, they would never have believed in Christ nor become his followers . . . The sum of religion to the true Christian is to know the voice of Christ within him and to follow him in everything . . . The priests deceive the people that eternal life is in the sacraments, but these have not believed God's witness in His son.'

A new excitement surged through Rowland Ellis as he listened to his servant. Did Ellis have an idea of the true significance of his words? He could not be sure, but the boy had a remarkable memory and he had remembered every single word Ifan Robarts had told him.

'Our ears have been deafened by theological arguments. Our eyes have been blinded by church ritual. In his despair George Fox heard a voice which said to him, "There is one, even Christ Jesus, that can speak to thy condition", and his heart leapt with joy. The Lord revealed to him that the light is to be found in the communion of the spirit with God Himself, for the light doth light a secret room in the heart of every man.'

Ellis spoke of the love of Christ, of truth, of steadfastness and

tenderness as he had understood the words, and Rowland marvelled at what came from the lips of this unlettered boy. He went
on to speak of the nature of Quaker meetings and of the silence
which sometimes lasted the whole meeting through.

They had reached the gate of Bryn Mawr before realising they
were home.

For the first time in her life Meg felt unsure of herself; ever since
the Plygain at Hengwrt, in fact. Until now, she had always been
able to predict her husband's exact reaction to whatever she did or
said, and this had stood her in good stead in the past. She had
always been able to tread the provocative path of the natural flirt,
without ever falling over the precipice of indiscretion. That jealousy is an oil that can inflame love she knew intuitively.

What irritated her was that worse had happened in the past than
had occurred at Hengwrt. For the hundredth time her mind went
over the events of that night. Hywel Vaughan had been particularly attentive, true. They had had their fill of wine but not as much
as most of the other guests. Was it not said afterwards that about
twenty of them had slept under the tables in the dining hall and
that those who had managed to reach St. Mary's Church had set
the altar cloths on fire with their candles? Very well. Why then
that distracted look in Rowland's eyes?

All he had seen was Hywel trying to draw her aside for a kiss.
But he had seen that sort of thing dozens of times before during the
Merry Nights and dances and feasts they had attended together.
What was in a kiss?

Ann started to cry again. Impatiently Meg thrust out a foot to
rock the cradle and almost overturned it. The baby's crying rose to
a shriek.

'Oh, drat it,' shouted Meg. 'Malan, come and look after this
child. I'm off for a ride on Barnabas.'

She did not wait to saddle the horse. She knew how to handle
him. In the open air, the cold wind struck her face and this gave
her a sensual pleasure. Barnabas started to trot towards the moor
but, as if sensing the excitement from his mistress's taut nerves,
he began to canter and then to gallop. On and on, faster and faster

went the two until sweat dripped from the horse's flanks. But Meg kept urging him on, her hair like black smoke in the wind, her voice rising all the time.

Slowly her self-confidence began to return. This was just a temporary upset. She could win Rowland over once again just as she had mastered Barnabas tonight. All she must do was be very, very tender for a while to allow the wound, if indeed there was a wound, to heal itself, however slowly. Patience. She must be patient. And take care to be more discreet next time.

For a moment, it did occur to Meg that there should be no next time. But away with such a notion. Flirting with men was as natural to her as sleeping and eating. She knew how far to go.

She was not a whore like Sir Lewis Prys's wife, ready to take every liveried servant into her bed. All she wanted was a little attention, and the more there were prepared to give it her the better. Rowland should be proud of the way so many men admired her.

'Home, Barnabas!'

She was anxious to see Rowland, to prove to herself that all was as before between them and that she was still mistress over him. She turned the horse around and soon they were climbing back to Bryn Mawr.

A lamp was burning in the stable, and Meg supposed that Rowland had gone to see that all was well before retiring for the night. But there was no one there but the servant, Huw Morris .

It did flash through her mind that Huw was uncommonly conscientious to be working in the stable at that time of a winter's night, but she was glad to see him. She would not have to go to the bother of finding someone to attend to Barnabas.

Huw was waiting for his mistress. He had been surprised to find Barnabas out and had decided to stay in the stable until horse and rider returned. Bits and pieces of information about this and that could come in handy at times and Huw Morris had a memory as tightly packed as a full barn. He would dearly love to know what had sent the mistress of Bryn Mawr out that night.

He rose to his feet slowly, straightened his back and thrust out his chest, as always when he found himself in the company of a pretty woman, whatever her station. He could boast that his muscles were the wiriest in the district.

But although his shoulders and arms were mighty, his body tapered down towards the legs. In a year or two the beer and mead he swallowed day and night would thicken him and make him heavy. But that time had not come yet. Just now, it was not only Nans y Goetre who looked at him and yearned to feel his brawny arms around her.

'Huw, take Barnabas,' commanded Meg. 'He's soaking with sweat.'

'You've ridden him hard, Mistress,' said Huw slowly with a smile. What a woman this was—his sort. Didn't give a damn for anyone. He held up the lamp to inspect the horse. My God! Something must have made her furious tonight. It was not Huw Morris's way to ask the direct question but he was filled with curiosity. He could see that Meg was in a hurry to reach the house.

'Perhaps I'd better come with you, Mistress. It's a black night and I have a lamp.'

Her eyes were accustomed to the dark by now but Meg allowed him to lead her across the yard. Huw searched around for a way of questioning her.

'The master's not returned yet,' he ventured in his low voice.

'Not yet?' Meg could not hide her surprise.

'No. Must say I was rather surprised too. He's not usually as late as this, is he?'

Having set the ball in motion, Huw waited for her play.

'No. Well, he must have called to see someone in the town. Thank you, Huw. I can see quite well now!'

But the servant took no notice.

'It's funny. I saw him going towards Brithdir, so he couldn't have been going towards the town. Not with that big bag, at any rate.'

What had Huw Morris got up his sleeve? He was obviously hinting at something. Meg was torn between curiosity and her desire to retain her dignity as the mistress of the house. Curiosity won.

'A bag?'

'Yes. Full of things from the larder.'

Huw knew that the arrow had reached its target.

He shrugged his shoulders and said quickly, 'But there you are. It's none of my business. Good night, Mistress.'

'Huw Morris!' The words were like a snake's tongue through the air. 'What exactly did you see?'

Huw smiled to himself but pretended to look uncomfortable.

'No, Mistress. I can see I've said too much already.'

The truth was he had nothing more to say. All he had seen was Rowland Ellis going to the larder, filling his bag with eggs and flour and cheese . . . He had followed his master as far as the bottom of Bwlch Coch but had lost him in the darkness, and, much to his disappointment, had had to return.

For the first time in her life, Meg knew what it was to feel jealousy concerning her husband. But fie, perhaps he had taken the gifts to a needy family. If so, why had she not been told? Why did he not send one of the servants? Where would he be going so late at night and so secretly? Only a few weeks ago the notion of her husband turning to another woman would have been laughable. But the Rowland who had been living with her since Christmas was not the same Rowland that she had known in the past. She did not know what was in the mind of this stranger.

Meg had a great urge to box Huw Morris's ears for saying so much and then no more. With an effort she managed to curb her feelings and entered the house without another word.

She climbed the stairs without even going into the kitchen to see if Malan was there and that everything was all right with Ann. First she had to have time to gain her composure. She half hoped that Rowland would have arrived home before her and that she would find him upstairs already. But of course he was not there. She threw herself on the bed but the tears of self-pity would not come as she wanted them to. She could not keep still. Rising irritably, she went over to the window but there was nothing to be seen except the mocking movement of the bare branches swaying in the wind.

Meg started to listen to the ticking of the clock until the sound tore at her nerves. At last she decided to go downstairs, and it was then that she heard the latch of the front door being lifted.

As Rowland came into the house he realised that Meg had not

once entered his thoughts during the last four hours. His immediate regret made his greeting to her warmer than usual. Meg at once took this to be a sign that he felt guilty at having been somewhere he ought not to have been.

She stood on the bottom step of the stairs looking at him coldly, but his mind was in such a turmoil that he did not notice her expression. Taking off his cloak, he went into the room. He felt no fatigue after the walk over the moors with Ellis, and his mind was clear and sharp. Sitting down on the settle he began to take off his boots.

How he loved the hills and pastures surrounding Bryn Mawr. He felt his heart swell with an intensity of emotion. He loved them in rain, mist, sunshine or darkness . . . perhaps in the darkness best of all. By sensing the land rather than seeing it, he could become one with the earth around him. Was that the way of the Quakers— to feel the presence of God rather than to seek it with the aid of visible, tangible devices? He pondered on this in the middle of removing his second boot. The key was to hand but he could not yet open the door. Would his love for this new-found truth be greater than his love for his land—should the time ever come when he had to choose?

He sat, as if in a dream, one foot resting on the knee of the other leg, the boot fallen unheeded to the floor. Meg was afraid for a moment as she watched him. His eyes were shining as if he had a fever. She knew that he had forgotten her yet again. Was he becoming mad?

That sort of thing could happen very quietly, almost without anyone noticing, as with her Uncle Lloyd when he kept telling everybody that his servant had stolen money from him. Everyone believed him at first until the same thing happened with six of his servants in succession. Then things had got from bad to worse. Finally the family had had to lock him up in a back-room of the house for the rest of his life, cared for only by his servants, in case the Justices took him away to the madhouse.

She had to be firm and strong, that was clear. Whatever worry was agitating him these days, she had to insist on having back the old Rowland she had known.

Trying to sound off-hand she asked: 'Have you been far?'

'No. Only to Brithdir.'

'To Brithdir?' Her laugh was high-pitched. 'Why on earth did you have to go there tonight?'

Rowland Ellis knew that the answer to her question would open a floodgate of recrimination, argument and entreaty. But tonight, even while he did not welcome it, he knew the time had come to face the situation. The time for evasion was over. Although he was still groping for the truth, he knew that at last he was going in the right direction, and there was no longer any point in hiding it from Meg.

'I went there to see Sinai Robarts.'

'The Quaker's wife.'

Meg loaded her voice with as much scorn as possible. The knowledge was no surprise to her, but she hated it with her whole being. She started to tremble. A hundred times would she have preferred to hear her husband admit he had visited a whore. That would be natural in a man; most of the squires in the neighbourhood did so from time to time and everyone, their wives included, was prepared to turn a blind eye to it. But Meg knew Sinai and however much she wished it, she could not believe that her husband had made that visit for the pleasures of the flesh.

'The Quaker, as you call him, is dead, Meg.'

'So much the better, I would say. I can't bear fanatics of any kind. A lunatic, that's what Ifan Robarts was, and I'm surprised at you for mixing with such people.'

Even in her anger, Meg was beautiful. Rowland knew that he still loved his wife, but looking at her now was like looking at a wild rose in the hedgerow. He could admire her beauty from a distance without wanting to possess it.

'I'm deeply grieved you should feel like this,' he said in a low voice. 'I know it's because you are afraid. I am afraid too, you know.' He corrected himself. 'Or I was.'

He rose and moved towards his wife to take her hands in his. 'Try to understand, little one. You are not really hard, however much you pretend to be.'

Meg pulled her hands away as though they had been scorched. Like a child she cupped them around her ears.

'I'll not listen to any more. Whatever happens to you, my name

54

is not going to be dragged through the mud. I'll not have every rascal in town laughing at me. It may be of little consequence to you, but I can't bear being made a laughing-stock of. And through no fault of my own—just for some stupid ideas in your head.'

How often in the past at times like this had Rowland craved for peace. How many times had conciliatory words come to his lips in order to put their relationship back once again on friendly terms, even though it had meant humiliation for himself.

But tonight conciliation was not as important as clearing the air between them. He had had enough of being dishonest both with himself and with her, even if this time honesty was going to hurt. He spoke quietly but firmly, and as slowly as if he were explaining to a child.

'I went to Brithdir to see Sinai Robarts. She is left with nine children to look after and one is sick to the point of death. They need help. I have asked her to send one of the girls here as a maid. She comes tomorrow.'

He listened to his own voice as if it were someone else speaking. He had a strange feeling that this had all happened before; he standing there telling Meg that Sinai Robarts's daughter was coming to them; she, chalk-white, facing him, her body as straight as a birch.

He heard her sharp voice speaking words which were familiar to him. Predictable words, he had heard often before.

'And this is the man who swore he loved me.'

Swift as a flame she snatched one of the red glasses from the dresser and before he could stop her she had dashed it to the floor in smithereens.

'That much for your love. If my wishes do not count for more than your sympathy for some half-witted hoyden, she's welcome to a share of your bed. But don't expect me to stay here too.'

'Meg . . . '

Rowland tried to hold her but his wife was furious. With all her strength she struck him across the face. For a second they faced each other, Meg with fear at having done something she had never done before, Rowland with sadness for a past that would never return.

5

But, in spite of her threat, Meg stayed at Bryn Mawr. That night, as they both lay side by side in the big bed, staring sleeplessly, unseeingly in the darkness at the carved oak posts and the curtains around them, Meg knew she had lost the battle.

In any case, where could she go? Home to her mother and father? But then everyone would say that Rowland Ellis had turned her out for misbehaving herself. And somehow the idea of returning to her home held no appeal for the lady of Bryn Mawr.

Here she was mistress, though not over her husband, she re flected bitterly. To London with Hywel Vaughan? The notion was attractive but she knew in her heart that the squire of Hengwrt was not the man to jeopardise his position for the sake of any woman. No, she would have to make the best of her life here— that's what she must do. She thought of the new maid she was expected to welcome tomorrow and was overcome again by a wave of resentment. What sort of justice was there in this world that compelled her to give shelter to the spawn of a sect of people she despised—simply because her husband insisted?

Well, we shall see, she told herself angrily.

Turning on her side, for the hundredth time she tried unsuc- cessfully to banish the other worry that had been gnawing at her during the past month. Fate seems to be intent on preventing me from enjoying myself and living a full life, she sighed with self- pity; my husband consorting with half-baked creatures, myself a prisoner in the mountains these past nine months and now per- haps to be a prisoner yet again. What will happen if Rowland is sent to jail like Robert Owen, Dolserau, and I with child?

If Rowland went to jail she had to be rid of the child. She would seek help. Betsan Prys had been the one for that sort of thing. She knew that Nans y Goetre had been to her more than once. But

Betsan was dead and she knew of no one else. Oh, well, perhaps there would be no need . . .

Maybe he had been impulsive in hiring Lisa Robarts without consulting Meg and, for that matter, without even seeing the girl himself. But it was too late now. Sinai Robarts had been so relieved, it would be cruel to draw back now. And as for Meg . . . he tried to tell himself that she would be pleased to have Lisa to help her once she had accepted the fact. But the memory of that blow across his face drowned all other emotions .

In the darkness his old self-doubt assailed him, shattering the serenity he had experienced only an hour before. Although the room was icy cold his forehead was damp with sweat and he felt the clothes around him like ropes binding him to the bed. In the distance he heard one of the dogs howling, a mournful cry echoing the anguish in his own heart.

Next morning Lisa Robarts arrived at Bryn Mawr. Ellis Puw had risen earlier than usual to go over to Brithdir to fetch her. As he walked back with her over the moor he could not help wishing it was Dorcas by his side. But he banished the unworthy thought from his head. The girl asked ceaseless questions about the mistress and the other servants. He answered her patiently and was relieved to see that for her this was a new adventure and not something to be feared.

She ran on ahead of him jumping about like a mountain pony. He laughed as he watched her, her black hair escaping from the unaccustomed pins put there by Dorcas to keep it tidy, her ragged shawl falling over one shoulder. How different she was from Dorcas. He thought of the older girl, grave and quiet as she cared for the houseful of children. But Lisa had always been headstrong, wandering over the mountains like a gypsy child, always arguing with her mother, and somehow living a life of her own, set apart from the family.

Having climbed the hill to Bryn Mawr, Ellis left the new maid in Malan's care. The old woman looked dubiously at the girl's lively eyes and apparent lack of shyness but said nothing.

57

The truth was that the old servant felt a little peevish, for the master had broken the news to her that Lisa had come mainly to help her look after Ann. She could not understand why it was thought she needed help. Even if her arms were old, the child was happy enough to sleep in them. Ann had been nursed more by her than by her mother, and she was overcome by waves of jealousy at the thought of yielding any of this care to a complete stranger.

What had possessed the master to hire another servant in any case? She was sure the mistress had known nothing about it until last night. And, goodness gracious, there was surely enough elbow grease between Cadi and herself to tackle any job on the farm. Where was the need for anyone else?

Lisa had never before been in a house as big as Bryn Mawr and she looked around with curiosity. There were strange smells every-where—polished oak, roast ham and new milk. Her eyes took in the hearthstone gleaming white from constant scrubbing, the oatmeal chest, the settle by the fire, the pewter dishes on the long table, the spit revolving slowly over the fire and the bubbling in the cauldron alongside. She suddenly became aware of a hollow feeling inside her.

'When is dinner time, Malan Parri?'

Malan looked at her scornfully. The question deserved no answer. Now that she knew she had been right in thinking the girl a bold, shameless hussy, Malan was mollified.

Meg had not yet come downstairs but Rowland hurried into the room to welcome Lisa. Since he could not be sure of his wife's attitude, Rowland showed special warmth in his welcome.

He realised at the same time that in doing so he was arousing Malan's resentment. She stood there waiting for him to finish, silent protest in every joint of her old body.

Poor Lisa, with two women against her already! But she looked happy enough bending down to stroke the black cat which purred as it moved backwards and forwards against her legs. He wished Meg would come down, but it was as if she were determined to ignore the new maid completely. She kept Ann upstairs with her and not even Malan was to be allowed near the child that day.

Rowland decided he must escape to the fields for some peace of mind. Drawing his cloak tightly around him, he took up his stick and called for his dog.

Sharing a loft with Malan and Cadi was a good deal better than sharing a house consisting of one room and a bedroom with nine others. Malan had a wainscot bed of her own but the two younger maids shared a plain wooden one. Lisa noticed with pleasure the warm clean coverlets. How different from the straw she and the other children had slept in so that Steffan could have one thin extra blanket.

Malan saw to it that Lisa was given plenty of work during her first day. She scrubbed floors, milkchurns, tubs, pails and bedrooms. She carried water from the well all day until her arms were almost breaking. But she was as strong as her mother had claimed for her and plenty of food did the rest. Lying beside Cadi that night she remembered with a little shame how everyone had stared at her at the supper table.

She had been so afraid her bowl would be cleared away before she had finished that as soon as the master had said grace she had started to bolt her food like a little animal instead of waiting for him and the mistress to begin eating first. Malan had given her such a nudge that she had almost fallen across the table. But the master had said, 'Leave her alone, Malan, the girl is starving. She'll be better tomorrow.'

But Lisa would not soon forget the look on her mistress's face. Meg's first appearance was at the supper table and Lisa marvelled at her beauty. Her skin was like buttermilk and her eyes like black cherries. Lisa remembered her father once telling her the story of Pwyll and Rhiannon and she felt sure that this was how Rhiannon must have looked. She would like to see her mistress astride a white horse . . . but the food had arrived on the table and Lisa forgot her romantic imaginings.

It was after she had recovered from Malan's jolt that she noticed the expression on her mistress's face. She had never before seen such a look of scorn. The next thing she knew was that her mistress had risen and swept out of the room, banging the door behind her.

Not a word was uttered in the meantime and this was hardest of all for Lisa to bear. She did not quite understand how she had offended her mistress so much, and no one explained to her. The gentry have odd ways, Lisa thought to herself. But she was not one to worry about things she did not understand.

Cadi was beginning to snore so she pinched her sharply under the bedclothes to wake her up so that she herself would have a chance to go to sleep undisturbed.

'Cadi,' she whispered in the darkness. 'Who do you like best here?'

But the other girl just moaned sleepily.

Decidedly Lisa liked the master best of all. There was something romantic in his big sad eyes, his slender body and his deep, cultured voice. Come to think of it, a thin body didn't appeal to her all that much. Take Ellis Puw. Poor Ellis. No girl would fall in love with him—with his straight, wispy red hair, his round shoulders and freckled nose. Perhaps Dorcas loved him. That Huw was a bit of a fly-by-night and perhaps his eyes were a little sly. Suddenly Lisa was aware that her breasts must be as big as Dorcas's. Stealthily under the bedclothes, she cupped them in her crossed hands. With great satisfaction she felt them filling her fists.

The snow came during the second week of January. An icy wind swept down from the mountains and people told each other that it was too cold to snow. But it started to fall at four o'clock in the afternoon after the wind had died down a little. As lightly and as quietly as a feather it fell.

'Fine snow, heavy fall,' warned the old people, their blood running colder still at the prospect. But so far the fall had been slight, as if someone had scattered powder all over the earth's periwig.

Outside the big house in the valley a lamp hung over the open door illuminating the white crystals on the ground. The figure of a man emerged from the darkness of the bushes into the shaft of light. He strode purposefully towards the door, and was followed by another figure. The two of them went through the porch to the back of the house, obviously familiar with the way.

Before long others had walked up the path from the big iron gate and had followed the first men through the porch to the small room at the rear of the house. This room was bare, apart from a number of wooden benches and a table in the centre on which was an open Bible. A small company had assembled—Ellis Ellis, Iscregennan, his wife Lydia and his genial father Tomos; David Evans from Llanfachreth and his wife Gainor; John Harry the schoolmaster; the two sisters from Llwyn-du, Elizabeth and Margaret Humphrey; Marged Owen, Dyffrydan; Morris Richard, the tailor from Dolgellau and his daughter Siân; Lewis and Rowland Owen, Gwanas; and, of course, their hosts, Robert and Jane Owen, Dolserau. They had always met at Tyddyn-y-Garreg Meeting House but after the restoration of the Conventicle Act of 1670, giving power to the justices to confiscate land and possessions as well as to imprison, the Quakers knew that to use the Meeting House, which was well known, would be tantamount to asking for severe punishment.

They began meeting in one another's houses, not stealthily, but without announcing their intention.

If the Justices suspected that they saw the same people repairing nightly to Gwanas, Dolserau, Hendre, Tynclawdd and sometimes over the mountain to Llwyn-du in Llwyngwril, they could prove nothing. There was no penalty for mere visiting.

But during recent months they had had no need to be so secretive and this was a relief to those who remembered with shame how George Fox had insisted upon proclaiming the truth everywhere no matter how great the danger or whatever the penalty. After the passing of the Act of Toleration, Robert Owen and several others had been released from jail, and not before time for some of them, judging by the pale features and bowed back of Ellis Iscregenan.

Men like Robert Owen knew enough about the King to be suspicious of his motives, but it was good to have some respite from persecution. Rumour had it that Charles had already secretly become a Catholic, having flirted for years with Rome, and that this move in the political game of chess was intended to help him get the better of his enemies—and at the same time protect his fellow Papists.

But, in the meantime, whatever the political reasons, Quakers throughout the country, like the company in Dolserau that night, could meet to worship in their own way without fear.

Not a word was spoken in the room. Each took his place on the bench in silence and sat quietly, some with closed eyes, others gazing thoughtfully at the floor.

Suddenly the small assembly was struck by a strange sensation. As surely as if one of them had risen to announce the fact, they all knew intuitively that there was a stranger among them, standing at the door. Jane Owen raised her head and slowly a smile of welcome spread across her face. She nodded her head to indicate an empty seat at one of the benches. Rowland Ellis stepped forward and sat down. No one looked at him but the atmosphere in the room was as if the sun had shone in the night.

He did not rightly know why he had chosen to go to Dolserau that night. After supper he had found himself directing his steps from Bryn Mawr along the narrow wooded path past Pandy, up the hill by Tyddyn-y-Garreg and down again to the valley where Dolserau stood in the meadow by the river Wnion.

The snow had taken the edge off the bitter cold and the grey clouds indicated a further fall before dawn. Rowland hastened his steps. He felt a sudden need to reach Dolserau quickly. By the time he came to the house blood was drumming in his head, and he was out of breath. He saw the lamp above the open door shining its welcome and one by one dark figures crossing the threshold. He had stayed a moment in the shelter of the bushes but not for long. On he went to join the others as if propelled by some powerful force.

When he had entered the house he had been uncertain where to go. There was no sound, nor was anyone to be seen. But at the furthermost end of the hall he could see a light coming from the back room. He walked towards it, entered the room and found himself among the most silent group of people he had ever encountered.

He sat on the bench in response to Jane Owen's unspoken invitation, the beating of his heart and the turmoil of his thoughts clamouring fretfully against the stillness. He had the sensation of being odd man out in this assembly, excluded from a secret they shared. He shuffled in his seat and began to regret having come, for the silence was oppressive to him. To shut out the others, he closed his eyes.

In his mind's eye he saw his fellow worshippers. He knew them all by name, some better than others. The two brothers from Gwanas, Lewis and Rowland, both tall, thin and redheaded. The young Ellis Ellis from Iscregennan. He had worked with him at shearing time. His cousins, Elizabeth and Margaret Humphrey. He had not seen them for a long while. He had purposely avoided them. And another of his cousins, Marged Owen, Dyffrydan.

Nearest him was Morris Richard, the tailor. He had known this man since he was a child and remembered him always as cantankerous and unsmiling. At one time he had been one of the Fifth Monarchists . . . What had made him join the Quakers? For that matter had not Robert Owen himself been a member? All Rowland's doubts assailed him again. He recalled his unwillingness as a child to visit the tailor's house—the stone steps leading to the door below the street, as if to the devil's den; the peaty gloom inside, Morris's petulant voice and his clever hands, soft as the wool itself, measuring the cloth on him. And always in the background his daughter Siân handing the pins to her father, raising one end of the cloth so that it did not touch the earthen floor, and eyeing the boy with an intensity that sent an uncomfortable shiver down his back.

Rowland remembered how Meg despised some of these people who were there that night. In his desire to be sincere, he asked himself whether he was blaming Meg for impressions which he himself had hitherto shared. He made himself look at Morris Richard, and a wave of humility came over him. There must be some virtue, even if hidden, in Morris and Siân. Perhaps this was God's way of showing him that the inner light shone within each and everyone.

All at once he felt he knew the truth. The black cloud that had been hovering above him for months broke, raining a gentle shower of contentment over him. Gradually, he felt himself merging with the other Friends in their silence. The throbbing in his head subsided and at last he was able to forget his own body in the company around him.

'Oh, my brothers and sisters,' exclaimed a low voice within him, 'this is the hour to which my whole life has been directed. This is the true body of Christ. This is the true Communion.' Meg should be at his side sharing this spiritual union, for it had come to him suddenly that this communion with God was a natural extension of the supreme ecstasy between man and wife.

He came to himself gradually, as if from a deep sleep, to realise that someone was speaking. For a little while he did not want to listen. He was floating on the gentle waters which ran between heaven and earth. The waves were carrying him towards some blissful sanctuary. If he could only fix his mind and his whole heart on the quiet figure moving towards him on this blessed sea, the peace and tranquillity of spirit his whole being craved for would be his. But the image was receding and a human voice was shutting it out.

It was Robert Owen who was speaking. Rowland sensed rather than heard him talk of their joy that God had sent another to their midst. Rowland Ellis now knew that he would not turn back. Whatever happened, however many dangers or sacrifices he had to face, this was his home, here among these people, for the rest of his life.

6

On the first day of April in the year 1673, King Charles II was in trouble with the House of Commons, the Reverend Thomas Ellis was on his deathbed and Lisa Robarts was in the kitchen at Bryn Mawr playing hop, skip and jump with a pet lamb born the previous week. Lisa knew nothing of Charles's troubles, and it certainly would not have occurred to her that happenings in far away places like London—such high places, too— could have any bearing on her life in the Merioneth mountains. Neither did she imagine that the death of the Rector could be any concern of hers.

The wars of England and France with the Dutch lingered on, the fleet sinking further into debt day by day, with the result that Charles was obliged to ask Parliament for help. But this time Parliament had had wind of the King's true motive in consorting with Papist France. It was rumoured that the commander of the fleet, the Duke of York, was a Catholic. And had not My Lady Castlemaine, the King's mistress, been heard bragging shameless-ly about her conversion? If she, then what of the King? The reports spread and speculation mounted into one cogent question. What lay behind the Declaration of Indulgence? Did it not open doors for the Papists under cover of tolerance towards the Nonconformists?

Charles was called upon to prove his fidelity to Protestantism by repealing the Declaration of Indulgence and commanding all those in the service of the Crown to take an oath of allegiance and supremacy, to declare against transubstantiation and to take the sacraments in accordance with the edicts of the Church of England.

This had a startling effect. The Duke of York, Sir Thomas Clifford, Lord of the Treasury, resigned rather than take such an oath, proving how close the country had been to falling into the clutches of Rome once again. The Papists were driven underground and dissenters and nonconformists of all kinds looked to the future once more with fear.

But Lisa knew nothing of all this. She was particularly happy that day. The plum tree was in flower and she had seen a squirrel on the wall that morning. She had gathered a garland of violets, wood sorrel and vetch and Ellis had brought her a parcel from Dorcas. In it was a yellow ribbon for her hair, an apron with primroses embroidered on it, and a white lace fichu. She had often seen her mistress wear clothes that made her mouth water with envy, but it was she, Lisa, who owned these, the most beautiful things she had ever had.

It did not enter her head to ask how Dorcas had managed to send her such luxuries. Ellis did not tell her that Jane Owen had given them to Dorcas but that the older girl had insisted that her sister should have them.

'Lisa lives amongst respectable folk at Bryn Mawr. I never go anywhere for anyone to see me.'

Ellis refrained from saying that he saw her and that he wanted her to wear the yellow ribbon for him. Without revealing his true thoughts, he promised to take the parcel to her sister

Lisa was wearing the apron and had tied the ribbon in her hair. She had left the fichu in the box by the side of the bed. The Flower Fair would be coming to Dolgellau before long and perhaps she would have a chance of wearing the apron and ribbon at the supper table. She caught the lamb to her suddenly and nursed it like a baby.

'O, th'art worth the whole world, pretty darling. Rock-a-bye baby. Are the cruel ones going to hurt 'ee then? There, there. Give tha Mammy a kiss then.'

'I'll give Mammy a kiss, if she'll let me.'

Lisa jumped and let the lamb slide from her arms.

'O, Huw Morris, I didn't see 'ee. Tha frightened me.'

'No need to be afraid, little one.'

Huw Morris was standing so near her that the buckle of the leather belt clasping his tunic was cold on her bare arm. She wrinkled her nose at the smell of his corduroy breeches and the dung which clung to the bottom of his heavy boots.

'Give us a kiss, then.'

She shook her arm free of the hairy hand groping clumsily at her.

'No indeed. Tha'll dirty my new apron.' This was not the first time Huw had tried to steal a kiss from her and although she showed anger, she did not altogether dislike the idea. Nor did she complain to Ellis about him. He would have made a mountain of a molehill, and might even have told the master. If her mother or Dorcas had the slightest suspicion, then that would be the end of Bryn Mawr for her, so she had better remain silent about it and keep the distance between herself and Huw as wide as possible.

Surprisingly Huw obeyed, and did not attempt to touch her again. He went to sit on the settle and watched her prepare the supper table. During the three months she had been in service at Bryn Mawr a great change had come over Lisa. Milk and eggs and wheatmeal bread had done their work. The bony crevices in her body had filled out, forming her delightfully into half-girl, half-woman.

Her mistress continued to ignore her, but this no longer worried her very much. For that matter, the mistress ignored everyone, sitting in her bedroom for hours on end, or lying on her bed doing nothing. And by this time, Malan had accepted Lisa —grudgingly enough, but she now allowed her to look after Ann. It was as though the mistress had lost all interest in the child.

She knew Huw was staring at her. Almost unconsciously she swung her hips a little as she walked, and straightened her back so that her small breasts stood out high and round. And yet she took care not to go too near the man. He continued to look at her with a knowing smile, familiar with the antics of young girls on the threshold of womanhood, and leaned back, head resting on the settle, hands in pockets, legs wide apart.

Then came the slow, unexpected words.

'Thee'rt not one of them, are 'ee?'

The puzzled expression on Lisa's face was completely guileless. 'One of what?'

'Those Quakers—the Rab-siacas.'

Lisa put a jug of cider on the table without replying.

'Tha father was, wasn't he? I never saw 'ee at one of their meetings. Is tha mother one?'

'That's her business,' said Lisa sharply.

'Perhaps indeed, my girl.' Huw's voice was as smooth as goose grease. 'But I can't imagine a little thrush as gay as Lisa Robarts joining a sour-faced crew like that. We're here to enjoy this life, little one.'

Huw had risen and moved easily towards the door. Then he walked back slowly without looking at her. Suddenly he turned and cornered her behind the settle.

'Can I show 'ee how to enjoy life, Lisa Roberts?' he whispered, placing his big hands on her shoulders.

For the first time the girl was frightened. He pinned her back against the wall and she saw something strange in his eyes which made her afraid. She could feel his heavy breathing on her face and tried to turn her head away, but it was no use. His hands were moving slowly down her arms, his knees pressing, pressing.

'No!' Lisa pushed with all her strength but his hold was like a mole-trap. 'Huw, don't! Let me go or—or I'll scream so loud they'll hear me in Brithdir. Huw—' That very moment the house was filled with an unearthly scream—but not from Lisa. Huw jumped, back and, seizing her chance, Lisa ran like a squirrel to the door and tore it open. She stopped short at what she saw. There, in front of her, slumped on the floor was Meg Ellis, eyes closed, her white face so still, Lisa felt sure she must be dead.

'Huw,' she cried, this time clutching at him, her fear of the man overcome by this greater fear of death. Sensing the two staring at her, afraid, Meg moved her head a little and started to moan.

'What shall we do?' whispered Huw helplessly. He hated sickness of any kind. Half hopefully he added, 'We can't leave her here, I suppose?'

Strength returned to Lisa's legs. 'Master, master!' She ran to the door calling with all her might. But it was not Rowland Ellis who rushed in from the cow-shed, but Ellis Puw, his face anxious.

'Lisa fach, what's the matter?'

'Come quickly, Ellis Puw. I thought the mistress was dead, but she isn't for she's breathing and groaning. She's still lying on the floor and I don't know what to do.'

Huw had run out after Lisa. He was not going to be left alone with the mistress, and her likely to die on him. A feeling of relief came over him at the sight of Ellis and as soon as he had made sure that the young man had gone into the house, he slid round the corner and escaped towards the fields.

Ellis knelt beside Meg. The colour was returning to her cheeks and her breathing was more natural.

'Water, Lisa!'

'There isn't any, Ellis Puw. I've had no time to fetch any.'

'Wine?'

'Elderberry wine—and cider.'

'A drop of elderberry wine then.'

When Ellis had bathed her forehead and wetted her lips with the wine, Meg opened her eyes for a moment then closed them and started to moan again. Ellis put his arms about her to lift her up. Lisa stood ready in case he dropped her, he looked so frail. But the young servant was sturdier than he looked. He managed to carry his mistress to the fireside so that she was half sitting, half lying on the settle. This time Meg opened her eyes completely.

'Who—who is here?'

'Only Lisa Robarts and me,'murmured Ellis soothingly. 'You'll be all right now, mistress. I will go and fetch the master at once.'

'No!' Meg almost sat upright. She clutched hard at Ellis, then was overcome with weakness and fell back.

'No,' she repeated, her voice faint. 'I don't want him to know. Don't tell him—please.' Tears gathered in her eyes and ran slowly down her cheeks.

Ellis did not know what to do, but he felt sorry for her.

'All right, mistress. I'll not say a word. But you must go to bed and rest. Let me help you up the stairs.'

Meg shook her head and rose unsteadily to her feet. She took a step or two then faltered. She would have fallen but for Ellis.

'You hold her other arm, Lisa, and we'll go upstairs slowly.'

Meg was more composed now. She no longer protested and the

69

three of them managed to reach the bedroom. She fell on to the bed and moaned with relief at being able to lie down in comfort.

Ellis looked at her helplessly. Reason told him that he should tell his master without delay in case the trouble was serious. As if she sensed his thoughts, Meg turned to him with entreaty in her eyes.

'Ellis, I beg of you, and Lisa, too.' She looked around for the young maid who was hiding fearfully behind Ellis. 'Not a word of this to my husband. It's only—it passes. I've had it before. I'll be all right soon. I don't want to make him anxious.'

Ellis could see that her colour had returned, although there were dark patches under her eyes. He felt a great relief.

'Not a word shall pass my lips, mistress,' he said with a smile.

Meg closed her eyes again and Ellis motioned to Lisa to leave the room with him quietly. When the door had closed behind them, Meg turned on her side, staring with large, frightened eyes at the wooden chest by the bed. She placed her hands on her belly, and moaned softly.

'Oh God, what have I done?'

In the kitchen Lisa was beginning to get over her fright, and was full of curiosity. 'What was the matter with her, Ellis?'

'She fainted, I suppose.'

'But I often saw Mam faint. She didn't groan with pain like that.'

Ellis frowned. The same thought had struck him. A pity that his mistress was so stubborn. What harm would there be in the master knowing?

Although he was a farmhand and knew all about birth and death among animals, there was a streak of innocence in Ellis. But not in Lisa.

'When Mam was expecting she used to have funny turns, too, but only in the first few weeks. The mistress is showing already.'

'Be quiet, Lisa,' whispered Ellis, blushing.

'But it's true, Ellis Puw. Siôned Puw died at the fifth month. She miscarried every time and in the end it did for her.'

Ellis was disturbed. He knew how to cope with most illnesses, serious and small, but this was foreign country to him.

'Where's Malan?'

'In town. But in any case we're not supposed to tell.'

'Not to tell the master,' Lisa replied promptly. 'She said nothing about Malan.'

'I don't think she wanted anyone but us to know.'

'Well, it's her fault then, isn't it, whatever happens?'

Ellis looked upwards unhappily. The responsibility was frightening.

'I've an idea it's her fault in more ways than one.'

Huw Morris had an unpleasant habit of tiptoeing around the house, so that people would talk without knowing he was there. But Ellis remembered that Huw was in the secret too.

'What do you mean?'

The older servant grinned but said no more.

'Yes, Huw—say what you are thinking.' Lisa was full of curiosity, but suddenly Ellis did not want to hear. He knew that Huw was a liar at the best of times and sensed that he was about to say something unpleasant. He moved to the door.

'I'd better go and see if the mistress is better.'

'Coward!' But Ellis had gone.

'Tell me, Huw,' pleaded Lisa.

He laughed and caught hold of her hand. 'Th'art too young.'

'Oh, don't be so mean. Tell.'

He gave her a long look, teasing her. Then suddenly his smile altered.

'Dost'ee know Nans y Goetre?'

'The one they call Penny-a-time?'

'For shame on 'ee. Who told 'ee that? She's not as cheap as all that . . . '

'Well, what of her?'

Huw released her hand, and a wary look came into his eyes. 'No, not now, little girl. It pays to keep quiet about some things.'

'But, Huw—'

'No, Lisa Robarts.' His voice was firm. 'Tha can ask from now until doomsday and tha'll be no wiser from me. Not yet, anyway.'

Ellis had returned from upstairs.

'She's sleeping peacefully now. I don't think we need worry.

71

But—Huw . . . ' Ellis turned hesitantly to the older servant. 'The mistress doesn't want us to say anything to anyone about all this— not even to the master.'

Huw did not try to hide his smile. 'That I can well believe.'

It was the season now when days and nights were spent looking for young lambs, and tending them, the time of year Rowland loved best, before the trees were drowned in a sea of green leaves.

Day after day a warm damp mist shrouded the mountains and the sun would sometimes try to break through. He went about his farm with a lighter heart than for many a day. Meetings at Dolserau, Dôl-gun, Hendre and Tynclawdd in turn filled his days, and although he had not yet invited any of the Friends to Bryn Mawr, he somehow felt that Meg's opposition was not as vehement as before. At least, she said nothing openly. For that matter she said very little at all, but wandered round the house with rather an abstracted look on her face. She was not even interested in playing her harp.

He knew that pregnant women went through phases like these, especially during the first months, and decided to have a word with Gruffydd Owen, the physician. She had not complained at all, so perhaps it was just spring telling on her. Lisa kept out of his way for fear of letting the cat out of the bag. Ellis Puw hoped the master would gradually realise all was not well with his wife. Huw Morris had pondered on how he could get confirmation of what he suspected and then on how he could make use of the knowledge.

But Rowland was too busy to notice any of this. Ellis and he climbed the slopes of Cader Idris looking out for sheep that had wandered too far from the flock, and helped others deliver their lambs.

Malan was the first to open his eyes. The old woman came to him in the stable one morning and announced without ceremony, 'Tis time you got Gruffydd Owen to see the mistress or 'tis unlikely she'll go her full term.'

Rowland knew that the old woman was not one to get flustered over such things and he sent Ellis down to the town to fetch the physician immediately. Gruffydd Owen shook his head and ordered Meg to stay in bed.

'The child in her womb is alive,' he said in reply to Rowland's unspoken question when he came downstairs. He sat down slowly, and looked gravely at the young man.

'But we must thank God for that. Not your wife.'

Rowland Ellis felt a choking sensation in his throat and tried to swallow. 'I don't understand.'

But all at once he understood too well. She had never wanted the child. It had been bad enough before Ann was born but it was her freedom that was threatened then. This time it was a different fear. He had known this on that day a month before when she had accused him of making sure she would be captive once again.

'The father a prisoner in Dolgellau gaol and the mother a prisoner of her womb.'

Rowland realised he had been preoccupied at the time, had put the bitter words down to bad temper and had forgotten them.

'Doctor, is she . . . did she . . . ?'

'One day someone is going to drown Nans y Goetre for a witch, and indeed t'would be no more than she deserved.'

'But the child is alive you say?'

'Yes, thank God. Nans doesn't always succeed.'

When Gruffydd Owen had departed, Rowland went towards the stairs, but with his foot on the first step he stopped, then slowly returned to the kitchen. Malan was busy in the dairy and there was no sign of Lisa or Cadi. He had to have control of himself before he saw Meg. A wave of guilt swept over him. It is my fault for allowing this coldness to grow between us. She could have killed herself and I would have been responsible. Cadwaladr Owen had murdered his wife with a knife, like killing a pig. But I—I am no better, for neglect can be a knife as well.

If only they could return to the first days of their marriage when their lives were ruled by the five senses. The days when Meg and he could smile at each other—before that forest of steel had grown between them. And yet he knew wishing was useless, for no one ever gets back to the starting point. He felt a flash of hatred for this new light that had changed his life and was crucifying him. But he knew for certain that this same light held him like a moth in the light of a candle and that, even if it were possible, to draw back now would be a living death.

How easy it would be to go upstairs and say, 'Meg I know what you have done. I know why. Forgive me for my neglect. From now on my whole mind, my strength, my youth, my love, all that I possess are for you and for Ann and for the child in your womb.'

It would be so easy to say that today. But what of tomorrow? Tomorrow would cry out that this was not enough. Tomorrow would be empty without this new communion, this new compulsion that had entered his life and possessed him.

Climbing the stairs he decided to say nothing to his wife of what he knew.

7

Ten o'clock on a Sunday morning in summer. Every seat in St. Mary's Church was full, although the sun was radiant over the fields of corn, which was ripening early that year. If some thoughts wandered wistfully towards farms where scythes stood idle in the corner on such a fine day, not a sign was shown. Was it not decreed that every living soul should attend the Parish Church or be counted a traitor to His Majesty?

As for the others, those who were not farmers, a different kind of longing consumed them while the parson's fat voice intoned the never-ending prayers. Opposite the church stood the tavern, the Brown Horse, and the promise of enough barrels of cold ale to quench the thirst of a camel. Afterwards they would be in the right mood for the cockfights in the churchyard.

The parson would not be long now. You could always rely on him to cut it short, especially on a hot day with Ffowc, mine host of the Brown Horse, ready to open wide his doors. Morris Jones, the new rector, was a good sport, more one of the lads than old Tomos Ellis —God rest his soul—with his dry books, and manuscripts reeking of ancient worlds. At the end of the service this rector's feet would be the first over the threshold of the Brown Horse and his would be the first silver to shine on the counter.

Some said that Ffowc's wife and he—but that was gossip's talk, for sure, and the poor man only in town two months. What did it matter, anyway? Showed he was a man full of sympathy for human frailty. He and Hywel Vaughan were great friends and it was said that the two would stay up all night dicing with Price Rhiwlas and the squire of Caerynwch.

Well, only men like Samuel Ifan the lawyer, or perhaps those Quakers, would deny him his fun. Thank goodness, there were not all that many Puritans left. And as for the others, the Quakers, the Justices would have to do something about them sooner or later.

There was plenty of talk in Parliament that the Act of Toleration was a mistake.

Samuel Ifan, the Puritan, sat stiff-backed and dark in dress and countenance, every joint of his body registering disapproval of the rector—and of everyone else for that matter.

'Glory be to the Father, and to the Son and to the Holy Ghost.'

The words tumbled from the rector's lips and Ffowc the Brown Horse jumped up from his seat at the back ready to rush out and open his doors. But the usual ritual was interrupted by a shout from the doorway.

'Stop !'

All heads turned to stare at the unexpected intruder. Robert Owen, Dolserau, stood on the threshold, his hat on his head, his eyes aflame. He took a few steps forward holding up his hand for silence.

'Listen to me, dear friends, and listen with your hearts. What meaningless words have you been singing during this last hour? What empty words have you been listening to? Do you not understand that it is unnecessary to have this worthless ritual imposed upon you? Do you not know that the Lord dwells within each one of you and yet you are as deaf mutes in the face of His infinite love? When you leave this church you will turn your backs on Him, with your drunken roistering, your whoring, and your cruel sport. Here, inside this church, as you hearken to the empty prattle of the servants of the devil you are no better—'

The congregation remained frozen in their seats while Robert Owen slowly moved nearer the centre of the church, his great black hat still on his head. As the rector heard himself called a servant of the devil, he let out a shout of rage but it was not his voice that was the loudest. Samuel Ifan, pale as a stoat, was near enough to Robert Owen to strike him.

'Son of Beelzebub, take off your hat in the House of God!'

Stretching out his left hand he swept Robert Owen's hat from his head to the floor, then drove his right fist into the other man's face. This acted like a signal to the others and a crowd of people pressed forward to encircle Robert Owen. He did not attempt to defend himself as they caught his arms and ran him unceremoniously out of the church. He was thrown on to one of the tombstones amid a roar of derisive laughter. Slowly and painfully, he rose to his feet but by this time some of the Friends who had been standing outside the church had rushed to his aid. But he would have none of their help. He turned to face Samuel Ifan who had followed him menacingly. The two stood confronting each other. The blood rushed to Robert Owen's face and for a second the Quakers were afraid that he would strike the lawyer. But he closed his eyes for a moment and when he opened them again he was able to say calmly, 'If it be thy wish, strike me again, Friend.'

A thrill went through the crowd. This was better sport than cock-fighting.

'Give him a leathering, Samuel Ifan!' someone shouted.

Samuel raised his fist again and Robert Owen stood before him quietly ready to receive the blow. But it did not come. There was rage on the lawyer's face but he dropped his hand to his side.

'Shameless blasphemer!' he shouted. 'What right have you to speak for God? You insult him.'

Some of the crowd had started to mock the Puritan.

'Are you afraid of the Quaker, Samuel Ifan?'

'What about that blow?'

But there were others who were impressed—those who were seeing for the first time in their lives a man overcome his enemy without fighting. By now everything had become too tame for most of them. They began to lose interest and wandered away towards the road. For the time being, Samuel Ifan's face was saved by another commotion outside the church. Always looking for fresh diversion, the people rushed through the gateway, past the horses tied to their posts, and swarmed like bees in the direction of the cries. They were no longer interested in Robert Owen. The little group of Friends were left to themselves.

With her handkerchief Marged Owen, Dyffrydan, tried to wipe away the blood from Robert Owen's face. Rowland Ellis observed her composure in the midst of all the tumult. Some of the Quakers were obviously shaken but his cousin remained serene and practical. Robert Owen smiled at her gratefully and Rowland watched him with admiration. At first he had thought the one-time soldier cold and reserved. He rarely spoke and what words he did utter were always short and sharp like military commands. But today he had done battle in the name of the Lord. A soldier, every joint of his body disciplined to fight the enemy, he had stood there quietly with love in his heart—it was incredible.

It was not easy for a man with his background to forego his sword. But Rowland remembered how another young Quaker had once asked George Fox, 'May I wear my sword?' and how the answer had been, 'Wear it as long as thou canst.'

Robert Owen could no longer wear his either.

The sound of shrill laughter came from the common and then there was silence, broken by the voice of someone speaking in the distance. Lewis Gwanas strolled to the gate to see what was attracting the attention of the crowd. He ran back to the others, his face dead-white.

'Come at once! Something terrible is happening.'

'What is it?' asked Robert Owen.

'Siân Morris . . . Oh, come on Robert Owen. We must stop her.' The Friends followed Lewis Gwanas from the churchyard, and then everyone stood still. Siân, the daughter of Morris Richard, the tailor, was walking across the common, crowds on each side of her shouting, laughing and spitting. From time to time the tumult would die down while they listened to what the girl had to say before breaking out into jeers once again. During a lull the Quakers could hear her cry, 'Oh, daughters of Jerusalem, weep! Be aware of your sins of scarlet. For in the day of the Lord, which is at hand, ye shall be made naked and ashamed so that all shall witness your whoring and filth.'

'Merciful God, she's stark naked,' whispered Elizabeth Humphreys.

' . . . ye will be stripped as bare as on the day ye came from your mother's womb, as naked as I stand before ye now.'

The crowd closed in on her with one shout and some began striking at her body with sticks. The girl raised her head to the heavens and closed her eyes. Blood ran down the side of her mouth and an ugly red wound appeared on her forehead. Taking off his cloak Rowland pushed through the crowd with all his strength.

Hours seemed to pass before he reached her but at last he was at her side, receiving some of the blows intended for her. Somehow managing to throw his cloak around her, he pushed her slowly and awkwardly towards the tailor's house. At the door the crowd withdrew a little and a silence fell as he lifted the girl in his arms.

His heart was full of pity and yet he felt a strange sense of personal liberation, because for a moment he could believe he held in his arms not the limp body of Siân Morris but the body of Betsan Prys, the witch.

The sickly smell he always associated with the tailor's house filled his nostrils as he entered. Siân Morris was watching him with shining eyes which pierced right through him, but he could not bear what he saw in them and turned hurriedly to Morris Richards. The tailor, white-faced, was trembling all over.

'Jezebel. Jezebel—daughter of the devil,' he murmured through slack lips. 'Oh, the disgrace on me—the shameless whore !'

Rowland felt Siân Morris's skinny arms enfold him from behind and her body pressing against his. He heard her silly laughter and then from her lips poured a volley of obscenity against her father, such as Rowland had only heard from drovers. He tried to free himself but her grip was like a vice.

'Rowland Ellis, my dearest, my love.'

The words came like a kind of purring of a cat, more terrible in his ears than the cursing, but he felt completely helpless.

'Come, Siân Morris, someone must clean the blood from thy face.'

'Thee. I want thee to do it.'

No one had noticed Marged Owen, Dyffrydan, coming into the room carrying a bowl of water. Behaving as though nothing out of the ordinary had happened, she placed the bowl on the table and dipped a clean cloth in the water. Siân Morris turned her head for a moment and as he felt her arms slackening a little Rowland succeeded in freeing himself. He turned to face her, taking hold of her hands.

Morris Richard was so shocked at the way his daughter had abused him that he said not another word but just stared at her in fear. By this time Rowland had gained more control of himself, and

79

he said gently: 'There, Siân Morris. Go and lie down and let Marged Owen look after you. You must be very tired.'

Siân Morris gave a loud laugh, then looked from one to another uncertainly—Rowland Ellis smiling at her, Marged Owen quietly behaving as if this were all part of everyday life. A change had come over Siân. Her face puckered like a baby's as she fell to the floor and began to cry piteously. Rowland held his breath as Marged knelt to cradle her arm against Siân's head. But he need not have feared. There was a wholesome stability about the Dyffrydan girl which comforted Rowland as well. With a deep sigh Siân laid her head on Marged's breast and rested peacefully. In a moment she was asleep.

Marged raised her eyes and smiled at Rowland.

'Shall I carry her upstairs?' he whispered.

Marged nodded and between them they carried the girl up the dark, narrow staircase to her bed.

Everyone knew. From now on, the name of Rowland Ellis of Bryn Mawr would be for ever linked with the Quakers. To have lifted Siân Morris in his arms was as public a declaration of allegiance as Robert Owen's preaching in the church. The Quakers, too, now looked to him as an eventual leader and successor to Robert Owen.

Word came from George Fox that he planned to establish a monthly meeting everywhere and a quarterly one among the counties. Rowland Ellis found himself journeying throughout Merioneth, visiting Friends in Bala, Corwen, Llanuwchllyn and Llwyngwril. He went more than once to Montgomeryshire to seek the advice of the Lloyd brothers in Dolobran. Because he could speak English fluently, it fell to him to attend the special meetings across the border. Now and again English Quakers would come to Wales but almost without exception they would leave confused and disappointed because they had not been able to communicate with the people in their own language. Rowland had some difficulty in explaining to them that it was neither obstinacy nor discourtesy that prompted the people to speak Welsh in their hearing.

'Ignorance, of course,' the Englishmen would observe, grieving that the Lord's work should be obstructed by such barbarity.

'How is Meg?' his cousin Marged asked him one day.

Whenever he talked with Marged he found himself being completely open with her and sometimes after their conversations he would be surprised to discover some new truth he had not recognised before.

'She lives her own life, stays upstairs most of the time, sometimes goes for a walk in the evening.'

'She will be better after the birth of the child.'

'She hasn't much interest in anything at the moment.'

'What about Ann?'

'Ann is almost a stranger to her. It's Malan who looks after her.'

'Perhaps Meg misses thee when thou art away from home?'

'She doesn't say so—'

Somehow he did not feel embarrassed at discussing his wife with Marged.

'She has little regard for the Quakers.'

'I'm aware of that.'

'She's frightened of what might happen to her and the children if I'm sent to jail.'

'It's difficult for her, not sharing our convictions.'

Marged did not add that it was difficult for him, too, but she was filled with compassion for her cousin. What hope had he of doing the work he had been called to do when Meg weighed so heavily on his mind?

Meg had made her own plans. She kept her clothes and trinkets in the big oak chest in her bedroom. Rowland never opened this chest. It was Meg's, as the name and date '1670' carved on it showed. Every night for months she had delved through the garments to the bottom of the chest and brought out the applewood box.

She would open it and carefully place a gold piece on top of the pile which grew daily. This performance had become the highlight of her day. Sitting by her husband at table, with the servants around them, she would smile quietly to herself. She had a secret, something in her life not known to another soul, something that could buy freedom for her if ever the day came when she needed it.

She could think of Rowland—the husband who was prepared to risk his inheritance, the labour of his forefathers and the security of his wife and children—as a man who no longer concerned her. Only she and her secret were important and real. She was wise and had her feet firmly on the ground. If only she could be sure her husband would not be taken away until the box was full of golden sovereigns and until the child was born. Oh, God, let him not be taken until Michaelmas at least. The child would be born towards the beginning of September and she would have had time to regain her strength. By that time, too, the box would be full.

'Why does she smile like that?' ruminated Huw Morris. 'What's she got up her sleeve?'

Old Dafydd was teasing Lisa because she had tried to dress her hair on top of her head 'like the gentry'. Malan was scolding Cadi because the *stwnsh* was cold, and the master and Ellis Puw were talking together in a little world of their own, lost to the rest of the company. It was only he, Huw Morris, who had eyes to see and ears to hear. The information he had wormed out of Nans y Goetre as he lay with her one night was still his. It was time for him to make use of it. But what was that smile for?

Supper was late that night because the men had been out in the hayfields until long after sunset. All of them went to bed immediately after the meal so that they could be up at dawn next day. But Rowland and Ellis made for Tabor and a meeting of the Friends. Huw Morris, watching them go, saw them cross the stream at the bottom of the field and then went to the stable loft where Dafydd was already snoring. He listened intently for a while until he could hear the ticking of the clock in the kitchen even through the thickness of the wall.

Suddenly he stiffened. This time his sharp ears had heard the sound of someone's movements inside the house. He crept down the stone steps from the loft and drew near the kitchen window. He could see his mistress standing by the dresser. She was lighting a candle which she had placed on the dresser. He could see it all very clearly. There before her stood a box, the key still in it but the lid open, and inside was a leather pouch. From the pouch she took a sovereign. He noticed that her movements were hurried but neat, as though she knew well from practice what to do. Tying the pouch firmly, she returned it to the box and turned the key. The box was put back in the cupboard of the dresser. The key would no doubt go upstairs with the mistress to be kept in its usual place.

He almost laughed aloud. The mistress stealing from the master! Well, well. But why on earth should she want to do that? Rowland Ellis was the last man you could call tight-fisted. But what he had seen was a fact. Huw hugged his knowledge to himself. He could be very patient—must never upset the apple cart by acting too soon. Gently, he knocked at the window. He saw Meg freeze on the spot, but she relaxed when she found it was only Huw Morris.

She came to the door unsuspectingly and opened it for him. 'What's the matter, Huw Morris?'

'Just thought I heard a noise, mistress. And I knew the master was out . . . '

'Everything's all right, thank you.' But Huw had edged himself into the room.

'Are you sure?'

'Of course, I'm sure.' Her voice was irritable but there was a suggestion of guilt on her face. Huw sat down, resting his head against the back of the settle.

'What's the matter with you, man? Are you drunk?'

'I was never more sober.'

She shook her head impatiently. 'Well, it's late and I want to go to bed.' Meg placed a hand on her stomach as the child moved inside her.

'Yes, it's near your time, isn't it, mistress?'

Meg flushed, but Huw continued before she could reply.

'I'm sure you're glad now that Nans didn't manage it.'

Meg's face became as white now as it had been red before. She held on firmly to a nearby chair.

'Huw Morris, you *are* drunk. Out of this house immediately, or I shall call Malan.'

'I wouldn't do that, if I were you, we've got a lot to talk about. It's good sometimes to share what we know.'

It would be easy for her to call for help. But she had to find out first what he meant. He was grinning at her, not saying a word, leaving her to make the next move.

'Tell me what you mean—then get out!'

'Oh, there's plenty of time before the master returns.'

They were both speaking in whispers, neither of them wanting to waken the rest of the household.

'What did you mean—about Nans y Goetre?'

'Well, she's pretty good sometimes, although they do say it's a rough business. What a pity you went through all that for nothing, isn't it, mistress?'

Meg showed a certain amount of relief. If that was all he knew, what did it matter?

'What a good job the master knows nothing about it. You made sure we shouldn't worry him, if I remember rightly. Of course, as the husband, he should share the burden, shouldn't he? I've been wondering why you didn't tell him . . . ' Huw stretched out his legs and surveyed his muddy boots. 'But I can make a few suggestions. It's too soon after the first for a pretty young woman to be tied down again.'

Meg looked with loathing at the red face and slack lips.

'And of course a child can be born who favours the looks of another man rather than his father.'

So that was it. Meg began to laugh. To a man like Huw Morris that would be the most likely reason a wife would want to get rid of a child. The irony of it! What chance did she ever have of seeing other men, let alone sleep with them? All right, if Rowland had to be told by Huw, so be it. It was his fault that fear had driven her to do such a thing. And suddenly she was surprised at herself for having tried to keep the secret from him. Why should he not know—and suffer from the knowledge?

She continued to laugh and Huw Morris began to look perplexed.

'What were you hoping for, Huw? Why were you threatening me?'

Huw Morris realised he had made a mistake. He felt his hold over her slipping, and became annoyed. What right had she to laugh at him, the shameless hussy? Well, he had another card up his sleeve. The playful grin had given way to the hatred felt by a man jealous of the beauty and assurance of youth.

'You may well laugh. But what if the master should find out that his wife was stealing from him?'

Huw saw that he had struck home this time. He could barely hear her voice ask, 'What do you mean?'

'Only what I saw through the window!'

Since Meg did not reply Huw continued in a reasonable tone.

'I'm a wise man, mistress. The sort who knows when to keep his mouth shut if it pays him to.'

The light from the candle cast great dark shadows over her pale cheeks. He moved slowly towards her and thrust his face into hers.

'Go halves and I won't say a word.'

She raised her hand to strike him but he caught it adroitly.

'No, that won't do,' he whispered in her ear. 'Half, or else—'

'Half—half—of what—?'

'Half of those golden sovereigns you've been stealing. I know quite well that tonight was not the first time.'

Although he was guessing, he knew that this arrow had truly gone home. Her dismay was obvious. The precious sum upstairs cut to half! It would take her twice as long now to save enough money, and time was ominously short. Her golden sovereigns to be shared with this odious man who stood before her, his lips moist with greed . . .

'I have the right—'

'To come here slyly by night?'

He shall not share them. She felt sick. All those weeks of care so that Rowland should not suspect anything. How she had disciplined her urge to help herself to a pouchful of sovereigns at a time instead of taking them one by one so that her husband should not find out. Was this all to be in vain? No, by God, it was not! She must try every other way. Forcing a smile, she managed to speak lightly.

'Well, there you are, Huw Morris. You have discovered my secret. And I had hoped to surprise my husband.'

A sharp thrill went through her—a small ray of hope that she had made an impression on him. Her voice became stronger as she gained confidence.

'You didn't know, of course, that he has a birthday next week. I had intended buying him a golden goblet.' Meg looked straight into the servant's eyes. Her eyelids half closed as she whispered, 'You wouldn't betray my secret, would you, Huw Morris? I hadn't quite enough money of my own.'

He's not sure what to believe, thought Meg triumphantly, confidence completely restored by now. She rested her arms on the back of the chair between them, so that the candle on the side-table threw its light on her half bare breasts.

'You made a serious mistake tonight, Huw Morris. But I'll forgive you if only you'll let me have the pleasure of surprising my husband with my present. I shan't be able to if you tell him. Promise me you'll keep silent, will you, Huw?'

Her voice was like that of a child but her expression blatantly provocative. Mercy on us! Was it possible that the mistress was prepared to offer herself to him as the price of his silence? Did she imagine he was that much of a fool?

'Here you are. Take this sovereign to show there's no ill feeling between us.'

Holding his hand out slowly to receive the money, he said nothing but looked at her thoughtfully. Then he turned on his heel and left the room.   .

Meg remained standing where she was, uncertainly. Had she won? Gradually realising that the servant had in fact gone, she almost shouted in triumph. She snatched up the candle and fled upstairs. Quickly opening the clothes chest she rummaged among the garments inside, and brought out the precious box, the box that held her future. A sigh almost like a cry escaped her as she buried her hand among the gold pieces savouring the comfort they gave. She lifted a handful to the light. Tears of relief ran down her cheeks and she started to laugh almost hysterically.

'They feel good, don't they, mistress?'

The laughter turned to a scream which choked in her throat. The servant stood there, with his back against the doorway. He held out his hand. Then, as she opened her mouth to scream again, he moved cat-like towards her and placed his hand over her mouth. 'Your screaming will have woken the house already. We must have more time to seal our bargain.'

Huw had worked things out carefully. If he took all the money, there would be no more reason for her silence; moreover, it would be too easy for her to accuse him of having stolen it and his word would never be accepted before hers. Allowing her to keep half would leave the door open. He laughed quietly at the idea of the mistress and himself as conspirators.

'I'll be waiting for you in the kitchen in half an hour and if the master has come home before then, be in the cowshed tomorrow at noon. Half shares, remember. I'll know if you've cheated me.'

Huw Morris vanished down the stairs silently. Meg stared at the open box at her feet and started to tremble. Sweat gathered on her forehead and around her nose and lips. Suddenly she felt her body being torn by an agonising pain, bearing her down, down.

'Oh, no, not now! God, don't let it happen now!'

She tried to close the box and drag it back to the chest but the effort was too much for her and she had to let everything go. As she clung wildly to the bedpost, straining away from it, a great wet stain flooded the floor where she stood.

'Malan!' Meg screamed before she fell unconscious to the floor.

It was with heavy hearts that Rowland Ellis and Ellis Puw returned from Tabor that night. Robert Owen, Dolserau, had just arrived back from England with news of Friends there, news that was far from encouraging. George Fox had been jailed in Worcester and many other Friends with him.

Robert Owen warned the Quakers at Tabor that hard days lay ahead and that he himself had been told secretly that the Justices were preparing to throw him back into Dolgellau jail.

When the master of Bryn Mawr reached home, further news awaited him. His second child had been born that night— another daughter. But in giving birth to her the mother had died.

Part II

1

Ellis Puw waited two years before venturing to tell Dorcas he loved her. By that time even the least confident of men must have realised she would be unlikely to refuse. For the first time since her husband's death Sinai Robarts laughed when Ellis shyly asked permission to court her daughter.

'I don't know when we'll be able to marry,' he said in his serious way. 'But perhaps in about three years' time I'll have saved enough to make a home for us both.'

Conscious of the little family gathered around the mother, he added, 'Steffan will be stronger by then, I'm sure.'

A shadow crossed Sinai's face but she said nothing.

'And I can still help 'ee, mother,' said Dorcas, her cheeks rosier than usual. 'I'll not be far away—not ever.'

Sinai sighed softly. She thanked God for a daughter like Dorcas. For Steffan there was no future; she knew that by now. Every summer she had begun to hope as she watched him muster enough strength to play with other children in the fields and woods. But at the first sign of September damp, as the earthy smell of the cottage floor deepened, his energy gradually flagged. Like the leaves on the trees, his cheeks became flushed, and his cruel cough returned.

Steffan was not Sinai's only problem. Occasionally, very occasionally now, Lisa would come to visit them. But her mother sensed that each visit gave the girl less and less pleasure. Duty alone forced her to come. Sinai was sure of this and she knew that sooner or later Lisa would become tired of duty. There would be excuses that she was too busy with Rowland Ellis's children; and it was true that, since Meg's death, Lisa's main task had been to help Malan look after Ann and Siân. She did little milking or scrubbing now, and as time went on, with Malan feeling her age and unable to cope with the noise of children, Lisa had taken over the larger share of the work.

All this added to her sense of importance. Gradually she was taking charge completely and was often heard ordering Malan out of the children's bedroom.

'I've got to shout, Malan, to make you hear me, and this disturbs the children,' was her excuse. But the truth was that she had become jealous of anyone who threatened this little kingdom of hers. The fact that Rowland Ellis was so often away from home did little to help Malan's position.

During the eighteen months since Robert Owen, Dolserau, had been back in Dolgellau jail, Rowland Ellis had been helping Jane Owen care for the small company of Friends in Merioneth. What with additional journeying between Cerrigydrudion and Llangwm in Denbighshire and Nantmel in Radnorshire, and the occasional visit to London to meet George Fox, Isaac Pennington and the young cavalier William Penn, he had little time to think about affairs at Bryn Mawr. Lisa had complete control of the two little girls.

In a way this suited Malan quite well. She was now seventy and it was as much as she could manage to see to food for everybody. In spite of her complaints that 'that girl gets more waspish every day' she was content to leave things much as they were.

But Sinai continued to worry about Lisa. She had noticed that on her last visit the girl had looked almost too elegant, her old grey dress trimmed with a costly looking lace collar. Her mother had refrained from remarking on it but she suspected Lisa had been rummaging through her former mistress's clothes. Oh, perhaps she had been given permission, but Sinai was very much afraid that her daughter was threatened with pride.

But she managed to hide her fears from Lisa because she knew only too well that reproving her would only alienate her daughter still further.

At the moment Lisa's own thoughts were on May Day and the all-important question—would she be allowed to go into the town to see the maypole? She had not dared to ask yet, for she knew how reluctant Rowland Ellis would be to let her join in such idle revelry. But Huw Morris had been telling her all about the May night feasting and how by a magic charm you could tell who your sweetheart would be for the year. He had also told her of the summer carols sung next morning outside the houses, and how the maidens would dress their windows with lavender, roses and lilies. Sometimes, if the Puritans did not interfere, there would be strolling players from Shrewsbury or Wrexham, and to crown all the dancing under the rainbow-coloured ribbons of the maypole. Oh, if only she could go!

And what was wrong with a little dancing and laughter? But she did not dare ask Rowland Ellis. Instead she kept on pestering Huw Morris to teach her the movements of the dances until she knew every step. Then she begged him to teach her the words of the summer carol

The whole world doth love thee, the flowers
  doth light thee,
And Flora's thy friend in this frolicsome play,
And thou in thy dewey green jacket so pretty,
With buttons of silver in May . . .

What could possibly be wrong with words like that? Huw had hinted that he knew more but when Lisa had begged him to say them he had shaken his head and smiled his secret smile.

'I'll tell 'ee when the time is right.'

Why must she blush when he looked at her that way? Her flesh felt all prickly and she was furious with herself for behaving like a child. I don't even like Huw, she told herself. Sometimes she even hated him. And sometimes he frightened her, she didn't know why. He never tried to touch her; at least he had not since the death of the mistress. In fact, if anything, he had been curt with her. But somehow when he looked at her like that it was as if she were half-opening a door of a strange, disturbing room.

She tried to shut Huw out of her thoughts and concentrate once again on Midsummer Fair. If I said I was going to visit my mother, I could slip into the town and come back to Brithdir along by the river, past Coed Fridd Arw, she thought. I'd be only an hour or two late. After all, I haven't seen my mother for four weeks. The master couldn't object to my going to see her. That would be cruel.

Having placed the responsibility firmly on her master's shoulders Lisa was happy.

Escape was easier than she had thought. Rowland Ellis had heard that Jeremy Mellor, a Friend from Lancashire was journeying through North Wales. He had once heard Mellor addressing a yearly meeting in London and had been struck by the obvious sincerity of this countryman whose plain, simple speech was coloured now and then with down to earth sayings. Rowland thought the people of Merioneth would have much in common with this man, and so he had invited him to break his journey at Bryn Mawr. Having heard that he hoped to reach Bala by mid-day, Rowland set off on horseback to meet him.

From an upstairs window Lisa watched him go. Then she ran downstairs to the kitchen. She was on tenterhooks until she had made sure that Malan was willing to look after the children for the rest of that day. It was a slightly diffident Lisa who broached the subject, afraid the old woman might want to get her own back by refusing her request. Malan looked at her suspiciously but said nothing. It was enough for Lisa that the old woman knew she was going out, for she was satisfied then that no harm would come to the children, although Malan showed no sign of being pleased with her responsibility.

Although it was early in the afternoon, the town was surging with people. And more would arrive after four o'clock when the men had finished work on the farms. Everyone was moving towards the Marian Mawr and Lisa followed. She could smell the remains of the previous night's bonfires still smouldering even now.

Not far from the Golden Lion yard was a large stone, almost covered with oak branches. Here sat Robin Fychan, the blind harpist, the sweat on his forehead glistening in the sun. He had stopped playing for the moment and was gratefully downing a tankard of ale thrust into his hands by one of the bystanders. Lisa stared at him solemnly. She had never in her life seen ale disappear so quickly.

But she turned her back on him suddenly as she heard a shout behind her. All around joined in the cry as they watched a troup of dancers approaching. In front of the dancers was the most astonishing figure. Its head seemed like that of the ugliest horse Lisa had ever seen. It wore a red coat and yellow waist coat over voluminous petticoats.

'Hurrah for the Cadi,' bawled the crowd, surging forward.

But Lisa's eyes were not on the Cadi. They were intent on a huge pole at the forefront of the procession—the maypole. A lump came to her throat as she surveyed the miracle of colours. Suspended from the pole were ribbons of red, blue, yellow, green and white . Robin Fychan plucked at the first notes of the maypole dance and the girls and boys raced to be the first to grasp a ribbon; then backwards and forwards they danced, the boys crossing this way, the girls the other, while a complex pattern of ribbon began to appear at the top of the pole. Lisa stared at the pattern forming, like some iridescent snake. Oh, the beauty of it!

Nearer and nearer the dancers were drawn to the maypole as the ribbons became shorter, and closer and closer they came together, so that the laughter and shouting drowned the sound of the harp. But what did it matter? The dancers were familiar with the rhythm by now and it was no longer necessary for Robin Fychan to keep time. The long awaited roar came when every inch of the maypole had been covered in a multi-coloured jacket of ribbon and the dancers stumbled together, some of the boys stealing kisses, some making the most of a chance to pinch their partners in tender places; girls screeched like piglets and boys threw back their heads in laughter. Then everyone about turned to begin the unravelling.

'Well, I've never enjoyed myself so much,' said Lisa to herself, determined to be one of the dancers next time. She seized her chance as soon as the dancing stopped and rushed to take her place with the rest.

Her partner was a boy with curly brown hair, and she prayed she would remember the steps so that she would not make a fool of herself before him. But Huw had been an excellent teacher. She knew every movement. The boy put his arm around her waist and

95

an unaccustomed thrill went through her body. He laughed and released her. And now she had to weave her ribbon in and out of those dancers around her. She saw her partner in the distance and he winked at her. Someone trod on her toe and in her consternation she almost lost her place. Now she was back with her handsome partner. She shivered as he caught hold of her hand and pressed it. The ribbon tightened and became shorter while she and the boy and all the other dancers drew closer and closer to the maypole. She felt her breast press against his corduroy waistcoat and his hand become restless on her hip.

'Th'art a pretty little thing,' he whispered in her ear. 'Can I go with 'ee?'

But there was no time to reply. The ribbons were beginning to unwind and the circle of dancers was spreading out again. What would he say to her at the end of the dance? A shyness overcame her and she longed for the dancing to go on for ever, so that she would not have to speak to him.

But when the dance ended the young man gave a stiff bow and smiled his thanks. Then he turned to a fat girl standing among the spectators scowling at Lisa. He whispered something to her and together they went off laughing.

Lisa felt empty with disappointment. She prayed no one had noticed. What on earth did he see in a big, fat dumpling like that? She was sure she herself was prettier. Perhaps he thought she was too young, or perhaps the girl was his sister. But Lisa did not believe that for a moment. Suddenly she was aware of being lonely, the terrible loneliness one feels in a crowd. She knew no one cared a button about her. Tears blinded her as she moved forward not quite knowing where.

Another knot of people had gathered around a big wagon a little further away. As she drew nearer, she saw two men prancing on it like ponies, one of them dressed as a Fool.

Now and again the crowd roared with laughter or cried, 'Hurrah!' 'Look out, he's behind 'ee!' 'Box his ears!' and other shouts of encouragement, mostly in English, which Lisa did not understand. First she thought the two men on the wagon were fighting, but then one of them stepped forward and started to address the crowd in a tearful voice. The Fool stood behind him, imitating every gesture. She did not have to understand English to join in the laughter. Suddenly the Fool struck the other man's bottom with the end of his stick. The man turned as though shot and tried to hit out at the Fool. But just at that moment the Fool bent down and the other's arm went flailing through the air like a threshing machine.

Lisa, her loneliness forgotten, laughed till her sides ached. There followed some five minutes of hitting and missing, teasing and clubbing with the two finally locked together rolling across the stage like some great hedgehog, falling into the safety net at the side of the wagon.

Something else now drew Lisa's attention. A woman was lying on a purple cushion, her hair, the colour of copper beech in autumn, cascading down her back. Lisa was reminded for a moment of her dead mistress. Behind the woman stood a man singing to his own accompaniment on a musical instrument that was strange to Lisa.

She did not understand the words but it must have been a sad song, for the tune was doleful. But at the second verse the woman raised her head and sang merrily, her eyes teasing the man. That set the crowd laughing once more but this time Lisa could not join in their merriment, only gaze at them, perplexed. Now it was the man's turn to sing, with tears in his voice again. The woman responded as before, and so it went on, the laughter becoming more raucous each time her song ended. Loneliness overwhelmed Lisa once more.

'How much of that did 'ee understand, little one?'

She was surprised how pleased she was to see Huw Morris, especially to find he was alone and so not likely to leave her immediately.

'It was in English, wasn't it, Huw Morris?'

'Yes. Thee didn't understand much of it, did 'ee?

'Did thee?'

'Enough.'

'Well, then, why was everyone laughing?'

Huw began to shake with laughter but did not reply.

'Huh! 'Ee didn't understand, else 'ee'd tell me,' Lisa flashed. But that did not work. Huw caught her by the arm and asked her to go with him to the Golden Lion.

'There's cock-fighting in the courtyard.'

This again was something new, although she had often listened to Huw's vivid descriptions of it, in spite of the master's warning that he was not to mention the subject at Bryn Mawr.

To reach the cockpit they had to go through the inn, where Huw insisted on buying Lisa a tankard of ale before finding a place for them both to watch the fight. She had never in her life seen such a big tankard and wondered how on earth she was going to drink it all. But she said nothing in case Huw thought her a child. She would teach him not to treat her like that. The sky was sea-green above the scarlet of the setting sun, the air clear and clean. But in the courtyard of the Golden Lion, people were in no mood to appreciate the beauties of nature, nor were they aware of the mingled smells of men's bodies, horse dung and stale beer. Aching feet, the long journey home and tomorrow's labours, all were forgotten. Every eye was fixed on the two fierce cockerels facing each other in the pit.

After a few minutes, Lisa tried not to look, but her eyes were drawn back time and again. As she watched one cockerel viciously tear the other apart, she felt a mixture of horror and pleasure—an unclean, ugly pleasure, but exciting . . .

She glanced at Huw but he was on his feet with the others—shouting, urging and swearing. The end came too quickly to please the crowd. The weaker bird had succumbed, its eyes and entrails scattered all over the pit. The victor ran wildly from side to side. The crowd screamed that it had not had its money's worth.

''Tis time I went home, Huw Morris.'

She plucked at his sleeve to draw his attention but he shook himself free impatiently.

'Don't be daft. The fun's just starting.'

'I'd thought to go and see Mam. No one knows I'm here.'

'Nonsense! No one goes to see Mam on Fair Night.'

'But I must go, Huw.'

'Stay for one more round and then I'll come with 'ee. It still gets dark early, remember. Here, let me get 'ee some more ale.'

'No. No, thanks. I'll stay for one more round, then—but just one.'

She was glad Huw had offered to keep her company. The men were beginning to look very drunk and the shouting had become frightening. At least Huw had not taken too much ale.

'Come on, one more before we leave. It'll do 'ee good. I promise we'll go then. Cross my heart, prepare to die.'

Huw crossed himself and squeezed her hand. In spite of herself she had to laugh.

'All right, then. But remember to keep tha word afterwards, Huw Morris.'

2

The wide valley of Garneddwen lay behind them now. As they followed the river Wnion on its winding way towards the west, Rowland allowed his thoughts to be lulled for a moment by the peacefulness around them. The candles of the horsechestnut swayed in the breeze above a carpet of bluebells. The thrush had started its evening song and the river chattered its counterpoint to the clatter of the horses' hooves.

How much did the beauty of the landscape mean to Jeremy Mellor? Rowland glanced at him and sensed the distance between them, although the flanks of their horses were almost touching. Mellor rode more like a farmer than a huntsman— carefully, slowly, his head sunk on his chest. He was not one to waste words. Rowland had already discovered this and had not attempted to make conversation. Half an hour earlier he had mentioned that Arenig Fawr was to the right and Aran Benllyn to the left but he had soon realised that the thoughts of this man from Lancashire were upon mountains less tangible than those of Merioneth, and had fallen silent.

Rowland was free to let his own thoughts wander. As always a vision of Meg came before his eyes, not the sullen, silent Meg of the months before her death, but the earlier Meg, lively, bright and loving. Somehow it was he who had killed that Meg, through not understanding, through not being able to explain, through ignoring her. No, that was not fair. He had never been guilty of ignoring her. But could the clock have been turned back five years, it would all have been the same. The force that drove him was beyond his control. Only Meg could have changed the course of events, but it was too late now.

How sad that she had not lived to enjoy her children. But she had been one of those women who had little time for children. Did he, as a father, spend enough time with them? He suddenly realised that he gave them very little thought. Malan and Lisa were there to look after them, to wash their clothes and feed them and put them to bed. As for himself, he was so busy with Quaker meetings . . . He forced himself to face the fact that he was avoiding the company of his children. No, not his children, but his younger child, Siân. She was the innocent symbol of all the darkness that had descended upon him and Meg. She was the final cloud that had darkened their lives. What use his preaching reconciliation with Christ if he could not accept his own daughter? A wave of shame engulfed him and unconsciously he spurred his horse on to a faster pace, until he suddenly remembered Jeremy Mellor.

They reached Dolgellau as the fun of the Fair was beginning to wane. Some weary revellers were wandering tipsily homewards. Others stood talking in small groups outside the houses. The sound of tuneless singing and now and again a roar of laughter came from the brimming hostelries. As they passed by St. Mary's Church, Rowland noticed three men standing together, more sober than the rest. Their talk ceased as they eyed the two Quakers drawing near.

Jeremy Mellor had noticed them too. He pulled at his reins and much to Rowland's astonishment, dismounted and crossed over to them. I should go with him, thought Rowland, but he did not move. Jeremy Mellor had hardly chosen the right moment to start preaching. Who in his right mind would pick on the last hours of a fair? Immediately Rowland tried to thrust the peevish question out of his mind. Perhaps God had moved the Quaker to speak now. Who was he to question the way and time of the Lord? There were no signs that the Quaker was unwelcome. The three men allowed him to speak and listened attentively Then one interrupted him. The Quaker looked at him questioningly, for the man spoke in Welsh. By this time the three were in heated discussion together. Jeremy raised his hand and Rowland heard him say in English.

'Speak more moderately, brethren, one at a time. For the things of God are weighty, and you should speak of them with fear and reverence.'

He turned to Rowland, calling, ' I cannot understand the language of thy countrymen. Tell them to speak in English.'

One of the three was very voluble. Rowland suddenly remembered who he was—a thatcher from Ganllwyd by the name of Gwallter, one of a family of Puritans. He had little English and Rowland blushed with embarrassment for him as he tried to put his thoughts into words.

'But what is this light within?' His nose was about a foot away from Mellor's face. 'The moon is light, yes? God was making those, wasn't he? For what want we more light?'

Jeremy Mellor looked pained. The lack of communication between them was complete. But Rowland knew that Gwallter was not being irreverent. He was seriously groping to understand the meaning of these foreign words.

'Thou art right, Gwallter. The moon, the sun, and the stars, these are natural lights, they were created by God. But there is another light, a true light, of which John spoke; that is the Life in Christ, the Word by which all things are made and created.'

Gwallter had now turned his attention from Jeremy Mellor to Rowland, who spoke the language he understood. His little wren's eyes were piercing above his long thin nose. Words which had been long gathering force within Rowland Ellis were released like a flood.

'And this is the light that shines *inside* every man and woman, the heavenly light which enables a man to recognise the evil in himself and cast it out, the light which illuminates the secret room of the heart. We all have this precious gift, Gwallter, even the poorest among us.'

By now, others had gathered around them, but Rowland hardly noticed. For the first time he was preaching his message not to the eager, receptive ears of his fellow Quakers but to people who did not understand, who were indeed hostile to such teachings. He had forgotten Jeremy Mellor standing beside him. All that he wished for at that moment was to share with his own people the happiness and peace of direct communion with God.

'Be ye therefore perfect was Christ's commandment. Christ does not command the impossible. He came to earth to reconcile man with God, to restore peace among men, to restore man, who was created in God's image, to his rightful perfection. The Lamb's war is an inner battle; there are no spears, no axes, no swords, no guns. Repentance is Christ's sturdiest weapon, selfishness and pride the formidable enemies. Those who are most guilty are the priests and false prophets who deceive you and come between you and the Truth.'

'Papist!' shouted a voice from the crowd. 'The man's a servant of the Pope.'

'The man's a servant of the Father, my friend,' replied Rowland gently. 'You are blinded, my beloved friends, by ritual, sacraments, philosophies and scriptures. It is not thus that God's grace comes. Discard these trappings and bring yourselves naked before God in worship and sweet communion through the power of Christ alone, who dwells within each one of you.'

'Blasphemy,' mumbled an old man, but no one heeded him. The crowd that Rowland now saw was eager and receptive.

'It is not through catechisms and chanting that man discovers the true life; not through long-winded sermonising but in the depths of his own spirit. God asks for a sincere and simple faith, stripped of the mannerisms and hypocrisy of this world. God requires honesty and if we are honest in our faith, we are honest with one another. Search your hearts, my friends. You inn-keepers, serve the thirsty but do not make men drunk. You who organise fairs and festivals, see that merrymaking does not turn to destruction. You vendors of trinkets and fairings, do not rob the poor of their money by offering worthless objects. For the message we bring you, through Christ, is to be trustworthy, sincere, and above all loving.'

Rowland Ellis had never before experienced the thrill of having a rapt audience before him. He sensed at that moment the power he had over the minds of these spellbound people and tears of joy and gratitude filled his eyes. Was this how George Fox had felt when he had come to the town over twenty years before? And Martin Luther, John Knox, Bishop Latimer? God must have revealed Himself to them, too, in the same way as He was revealing Himself to Rowland now. Was this how Christ Himself had felt?

It was as if someone had poured icy water over him. Rowland's words floundered and he felt as cold as death. A voice within him cried: Here am I having just condemned pride and selfishness as the greatest enemies. But what pride is greater than that of which I am now guilty, believing that I can mould and shape the souls of men with my eloquent words? The devil lurks in unlikely places. And yet, he tried to comfort himself, if a man has a certain message to proclaim, he must believe his words come from God and not from the devil.

Jeremy Mellor had noticed his unease. Without understanding the exact reason for the young man's faltering, Jeremy had started to address the crowd himself—in English. Immediately the spell of Rowland's words was broken and some began to murmur and grumble. The voice of the Quaker from Lancashire had about it a flat monotony, and although his words were direct and sincere they were too emotionless for these Welshmen drunk with the sound of Rowland Ellis's words.

Someone slid to the front of the crowd and slung a handful of mud in Jeremy Mellor's face. His voice was drowned by a scream of laughter. Another threw a fistful at Rowland Ellis. He could have jumped aside to avoid it but did not. This was a just punishment for his earlier arrogance. The first stone was hurled by someone at the back of the crowd—another came from the left—then another and another until they rained on the two men like a hailstorm. A few of the listeners tried to stop the onslaught but it was useless.

Blood gushed down Rowland's forehead, blinding him. He felt a stickiness inside his mouth as it trickled from the corners. Jeremy Mellor was standing still as a statue, his eyes closed, his mud-splattered face streaked with blood. Someone had seized his big black hat and rammed it on the head of one of the horses. Rowland fought against an overpowering desire to take the nearest young hooligan by the throat. This lad was jerking backwards and forwards, his body shaking as if with a nervous tic, a silly grin on his thin face.

'This is how they go. Like this. Look, Dic!' He doubled up with laughter, saliva running down his chin. 'Qu-qu-quaking! Look, Dic!'

Rowland knew he could have knocked the fool unconscious with one blow. *Give me grace, O God, to accept this humiliation joyfully.* But for how long? He saw that the last stone had brought Mellor to his knees. Rowland knelt to help him and received a kick which caused him to fall on top of the Quaker.

'*Bobl bach*, but aren't they filthy? Let's give 'em a wash, boys.'

Rowland heard the shout, but, before he could move, the contents of a chamber pot were coursing down his head and face. Bile rose in his stomach as he tried to wipe away the revolting mess with his sleeve. As he tried to rise to his feet, someone gave him another kick, this time in the crutch. He bent double in agony and once again fell across Mellor.

Slowly, painfully he raised himself slightly to relieve his friend of some of the weight of his body. He saw with a shock that Jeremy was lying quite still, his face the colour of marble. Some of the crowd had noticed his ominous stillness and gradually the raucous merriment died down as one by one they disappeared.

Rowland closed his eyes and let the silent darkness sweep around him.

'Your friend is coming to.'

He opened his eyes to see Gwallter's face above him, full of concern.

'Are you feeling better, Rowland Ellis?'

Rowland nodded, murmuring his thanks and his eyes brightened as he saw Jeremy Mellor raising himself slowly to a sitting position. Not for the first time Rowland marvelled at his quiet composure.

Mellor answered the unspoken question. 'Tis not the first time for me, my Friend.' He gave a crooked little smile 'But this old body is tough.'

Rowland was filled with admiration for this man. He must be at least fifty years of age and yet could stand up to such a beating.

'Rowland Ellis, I must . . . ' Gwallter paused awkwardly. Rowland could see tears in the brown eyes.

'Rowland Ellis, tell your friend that I have never witnessed such courage. And if I was discourteous to him earlier, I beg his forgiveness now. It is not words that matter. Seeing the thing work does.' Gwallter turned on his heel as if unable to say more.

Slowly the two Quakers walked towards their patient horses. On the way to Bryn Mawr Rowland tried to convey to Jeremy a little of what Gwallter had said. But Jeremy Mellor was a difficult man to praise.

'It would be better for these peasants if they could learn English,' was his curt reply. 'Thou didst well, Friend, for thou wert able to speak with them in their own tongue. But sooner or later, we will have to break down these frustrating barriers between all countries, if man is to experience true communion with his fellows in the Church of Christ.'

Rowland sighed softly. The frontiers of the mind could be narrow in the best of men. But he was too weary to argue. Deep down he was aware that this would not be the last time he would hear such argument. He was glad to see the chimney of Bryn Mawr rising into sight beyond the hill.

The smell of the bracken was sharp in the darkness. Above her head she could see the new moon like the tip of a fingernail, and the boughs of the hazel tree whirling above her. But it was her head that was whirling, not the trees, as Huw's hand moved with unexpected tenderness to and fro across her forehead and down her cheek. Then the pale light from the moon was being suddenly blotted out by Huw's head as he strained against her, kissing her on the lips—a comfortable kiss, affectionate, like a father's.

She closed her eyes but her head continued to whirl. She had misjudged Huw. To think that she had ever been afraid of him. He had been good company for her today—kind and considerate. She liked the smell of his corduroy tunic. She stretched her body voluptuously, then raising her left hand to Huw's face, outlined with her fingers his forehead, his eyebrows, his nose, his mouth. Suddenly he closed his lips round her finger and began to suck at it. Lisa laughed. This was a new game. But Huw was not laughing. He was beginning to breathe heavily and Lisa felt his body become as taut as the strings of a harp.

'Th'art too heavy, Huw.' She was half laughing, half moaning, but Huw took no notice. His left hand had released her breast from the fichu which covered it and he had his mouth around it as she had seen the baby, Tomos, against her mother's breast. Lisa thought this very funny. Huw a big, grown man wanting to be suckled. She laughed again but at the same time she was beginning to enjoy strange, new sensations.

'That's enough, Huw. We must go.'

The game had taken a peculiar turn. It was no longer Huw who was with her but a stranger, strong and frightening, and she was imprisoned under his body. This stranger was hurting her, tearing her in two, not listening to her pleading. Suddenly Lisa was a little girl crying for her mother once more.

Rowland was surprised to find Malan sitting in the kitchen. He knew that the old servant liked to go to bed straight after supper, but when he arrived home with Jeremy Mellor, there she was sitting silently in the chair, her gnarled hands folded on her black apron, her cap awry on her head which had keeled over on to one shoulder. Even the barking of the dogs in the yard had failed to awaken her. Rowland touched her gently on the shoulder.

'Malan! We have company. Malan!'

The old woman opened her eyes, and, fuddled, rose quickly to her feet.

'Beg pardon.' She curtsied to Jeremy Mellor as she had been accustomed to curtsey to her betters fifty years earlier before the Quakers had frowned upon the practice.

'I was just napping.'

'Where's Lisa?'

The old servant hesitated a moment before replying.

'Out.'

'Out, at this time of night?' There was more surprise than concern in Rowland's voice.

'Out,' repeated Malan, shortly.

Rowland decided not to pursue the matter for the moment, but asked Malan to show Jeremy to his room. When she returned, he questioned her slowly in a low voice.

'Where did Lisa go?'

'She didn't say.'

'But it's almost eleven o'clock.'

'Yes.'

'When did she go?'

'Just after you went out.'

After a moment's silence, Rowland said: 'All right, Malan. Go to bed.'

The old woman was tired. Relieved that she could now pass the responsibility on to someone else, she went to her room without another word.

Rowland lit a lantern and went to the back door. He held the lamp above his head and hurried across the yard, but there was nothing to be seen or heard. He thought of rousing Ellis. He could wait for Lisa in the kitchen while Rowland searched for her Penybanc way. But it would be difficult to wake Ellis without disturbing the others and there was no sound from the stable loft. He looked at the clock for the tenth time and as he did it began to chime eleven. He waited until there was silence again and then decided not to disturb Ellis but to go by himself as far as the stream.

Suddenly he stiffened. A rat in the wainscot maybe. Or was it the latch of the stable-loft door he had heard? He crossed the yard quietly and called out softly.

'Ellis ! '

But if it was Ellis who had made the sound, then he did not hear, or pretended not to hear, Rowland's call. Rowland changed his mind about going to the stream and returned to the back door. It was then he saw the shadow moving inside the porch. He walked quickly towards the buttery.

'Lisa!'

The lantern illuminated every corner of the buttery and Rowland saw the girl crouched behind the door. He swallowed the sharp words of reproof when he saw the state she was in. Her eyes with black smudges underneath, were big with fear. Her hair framed her head like a hedge of thorns. She held in front of her breasts all that remained of the white fichu.

'Lisa, what art thou doing, hiding behind the door like that?'

Lisa stared at him as if he were a stranger.

'Come into the kitchen and sit down.'

It was like trying to coax a terrified little animal. 'There's no need to be frightened. Thou'rt home now. Come.'

The kindness in his voice had its effect. Lisa rose painfully from her corner and came into the kitchen. At once she looked towards the door, longing to escape, but Rowland put his arm about her shoulders and led her to a chair.

'Now then, Lisa, what happened? What's given thee such a fright?'

'Was it a fall?'

He tried again. 'There was the Fair, wasn't there? No, I won't be cross if thou'lt tell me the truth.'

She nodded slowly.

'Wert thou in any trouble at the Fair? Was there any fighting? . . . Well, didst thou fall on the way home?'

He felt unable to draw her out. Perhaps questioning would be better left until the morning.

'Very well then, go to bed.'

She jumped to her feet at once and ran for the door but before she could escape through it Rowland's voice arrested her.

'Lisa !'

She stood still without turning towards him.

'Has anyone done anything to thee tonight?'

Lisa raised her fist to her mouth to prevent a cry.

She started to run towards the stairs but Rowland got there first. He took hold of her firmly by the wrist and gently led her back to the kitchen.

'Lisa, look at me. There's nothing to be afraid of. Just tell me the truth. Who was with thee tonight?'

Lisa kept her head bowed but something in the quiet voice demanded a reply. She mumbled the name almost inaudibly, and this was the name Rowland had half expected to hear. A great weariness came over him. Why had he not foreseen that this might happen? Lisa had been in his care and he had failed her. He had been too busy with his journeyings to keep watch over those nearest him. The familiar feeling of bitterness again assailed him. Was this God's judgment on him for his failure with Meg?

He looked down at the frightened girl fidgeting uncomfortably in her chair, and bent to stroke her hair. Lisa burst into tears of relief. More than anything she had been afraid that he would be angry with her for going to the Fair and staying out late. As for the other thing, she knew that was a sin, far worse than disobedience or staying out late. But that was Huw's sin, not hers. Gradually she began to lose her fears and her crying stopped.

Huw Morris sat on the edge of his bed taking his boots off. Ellis Puw gave him a sidelong look. He recognised the self-satisfied grin on the burly servant's face. He had seen it there before but tonight it seemed intolerable, more insolent than usual in the candlelight.

'Had tha wench tonight, *achan*?'

Ellis flushed, his temper rising. Huw often made sniggering insinuations about Dorcas, without actually naming her.

'Come on. Let's tell each other, eh?' Huw was trying to tell him something. He knew that, But Ellis turned over on his side and drew the bedclothes up over his ears. He tried not to listen but Huw's voice could not be blotted out. To brag about his escapades was an essential part of his pleasure and to talk of his latest conquest, and in great detail at that, was particularly sweet.

'The thing is, once you've started them off, they come back again and again for more. But I'm one who likes to choose, see — 'easy come, easy go'—that's my motto for women. But there you are, this little one will do me fine for a time. Is her sister any good, Ellis Puw?'

Ellis bounded out of his bed, the sweat glistening on his body. He hurled himself at Huw and pounded him with his fists. Huw was in his element. He could have restrained the boy with one massive hand and thrown him back on the bed without effort. He stood over Ellis, his great body shaking with laughter.

'Well, b'God, how's that for a lamb turning into a lion? The Quakers are not so peace-loving, after all. Good for thee, boy. I like to see a bit of kick in a donkey.'

'What if I told the master?' Ellis was so short of breath he could hardly speak.

'But 'ee won't, will 'ee? Because her mam would have to hear about it. And Dorcas. And the rest of the bloody brood. And perhaps Lisa would have to leave here. Then who'd support her? Dorcas? No fear, it's all too much of a mix-up. Ee'd better face the facts of life as they are.'

Ellis would have liked to have been able to call Huw a liar, but instead he covered himself once again with the bedclothes. Huw Morris was well pleased with the effect of his taunting. He put out the candle and was soon snoring heavily, leaving Ellis to stare helplessly through the window at the north star.

Next morning Rowland Ellis summoned Huw Morris to the house. He had told Lisa to stay in her room so that she would be out of earshot.

Although he had little time for Huw Morris he had never had occasion to reprimand him before. The prospect of the peace of Bryn Mawr being shattered by angry words dismayed him. He knew full well that Huw would not take this meekly, especially from someone younger than himself. He longed for the confrontation to be over.

'Yes . . . master?'

The pause between the two words indicated that Huw knew what to expect and was ready for it. Rowland came straight to the point.

'Thou wert with Lisa last night.'

'Well?'

'Thou didst her a great evil.'

Huw Morris gave him a long, curious look. Then he slowly wiped his nose with the back of his hand.

'It all depends on what y'mean by evil. I walked home with her from the Fair.'

'And let her arrive home in a sorry state? Don't lie, Huw Morris. To violate a girl is a grave sin, especially one as young and innocent as Lisa.'

Huw smiled very slightly and said almost kindly: 'Ye're a clever man, master, ye've read a lot and think deeply. But ye don't know a thing about women—nor men, for that matter. I'll tell ya something. Little Lisa enjoyed herself as much as I did. Oh, maybe I was the first, but there'll be others—many others. A taste before the meal, that's what I am, that's all. I know her sort only too well. Now, can I go back to my work?'

Without waiting for an answer, he was half way to the door.

'Stay where thou art!'

Rowland Ellis had never been challenged like this before and he was shaken by the experience. His own voice sounded unfamiliar to him as he said: 'It's all very simple for thee, isn't it, Huw Morris? To fancy a girl and take her—then justify it all by discovering in her the same inclinations as thine own. Thou'rt too accustomed to the ways of Satan to recognise that there are some things which remain pure and inviolate. Or at least until someone like Huw Morris comes along to defile them. Hadst thou shown the slightest shame or repentance, I'd have forgiven thee but since thou art so manifestly in the clutches of the devil, I must order thee to leave.'

Huw stared at him as if Rowland Ellis has taken leave of his senses.

'Send me away? For God's sake why?' It was now Huw Morris's turn to look shaken. He started to laugh uneasily.

'But what if every master turned his servant away for lying with a maid? There'd be no servants left in the land. Eunuchs. That's all. Half men, like Ellis Puw and—'

He stopped without finishing the sentence, spluttering with anger. He saw the look on Rowland Ellis's face but was past caring.

'Ye might just as well stop looking like God on the Day of Judgment. Ye know nothing about life. Ye know nothing about people. Ye don't know anything about what's going on under your very nose. Ye didn't know, did ye, that the mistress had been stealing from ye so that she could save enough money to leave ye. Ye didn't know that she—'

'Enough of that, you impudent liar!'

Rowland pressed his fists tightly to his sides and dug his nails into the cloth of his coat. I will not hit him. The words rolled round and round in his brain. A black hate vibrated through him, such a hate he did not know could exist.

He closed his eyes tightly and prayed for strength as he had never prayed before.

When he opened his eyes, Huw Morris had gone.

3

George Fox was released in February of the year 1675 having spent fourteen years in Worcester jail. Quakers from all parts of the country had come to the Yearly Meeting in London to greet him. Among them was Rowland Ellis, whose main intention was to let the English Quakers know of the growing dangers facing Friends in Merioneth.

The old man, Robert Owen, Dolserau, was still in Dolgellau jail, this being the second year of his second sentence. Jane, his wife, had been fined twenty pounds for holding Quaker meetings at her home. The justices had confiscated six sheep from Ellis Ellis, Iscregennan, because he had refused to pay tithes. For interrupting the Parson's sermon at St. Mary's Church, John Harry, the schoolmaster, from Llanfachreth, and David Evans, from the town, had been placed upside down in the stocks for twelve hours. And he had many other instances to report.

But the story was the same in England, from Carlisle to Plymouth. Everybody sensed that the days of toleration were over and that a period of greater tribulation than ever before awaited them. These dangers drew the Quakers closer together and they decided to hold weekly meetings for Sufferings, to consider reports of the troubles of Quakers in Wales, England and overseas.

Rowland Ellis wrote to Margaret Owen, Dyffrydan:
London 7. viii: 1675

Dear Cousin, I had no opportunity before leaving of thanking thee for thy great kindness to the children. Ann enjoyed her stay at Dyffrydan, and especially the rowing on Cregennan. She never tires of talking about 'the big water' and 'Uncle William', and I saw roses in Siân's cheeks for the first time. I fear, however, it will be a long time before she achieves her sister's robustness.

I was at the Yearly Meeting today and there was a fervent welcome for G.F. I had only a child's memory of him until I met him today. He is a big man, of such pallor as bears testimony to his long imprisonment. He has the long fine nose of an aesthete, a broad mouth and eyes that pierce through one. I can well understand why a man once cried, 'Turn those eyes away,' as he felt that look upon him.

Beside him sat a well-looking man—one whose appearance was vastly different from that of the rest of us. I was surprised at the richness of his clothing. His silk waistcoat stood out against the greyness and sobriety of our attire. Round his neck he wore a collar of delicate lace and ruffles of the same material at his wrists. His hair was longer and more fashionably tended than ours and his whole demeanour indicated that he belonged to the gentry. Thou hast guessed, I'm sure, that this was Wm. Penn, son of Admiral Sir William Penn.

I had better opportunity of appraising him when he rose to speak. His voice was the first thing that struck me. Its tone was cultured, accustomed to speaking the poetry of Milton and the prose of Jeremy Taylor. A voice used to academic debate and legal discourse. And his accent was very different from that of the countryman from Leicestershire.

Woudst thou have me name other differences between him and G.F.? While George Fox's eyes are peculiarly penetrating, Penn's eyes are large and thoughtful. Whereas the one face shows the strength of a practical man of considered speech, the other displays perhaps a certain immaturity, a certain sensuousness of mouth. And yet some indescribable quality unites these unlikely two. Hast thou heard how Penn has been jailed time and time again, the last time at Newgate, that most cruel and most filthy of prisons? I heard yesterday of his courage and skill at the Old Bailey when he pleaded his own cause. The jury found him not guilty, but Recorder Hywel refused to accept their verdict. He ordered them to be confined to a room without food or drink, warmth or tobacco until they had pronounced Penn and his friend, William Mead, guilty. 'You are Englishmen,' Penn said to the jury. 'Guard your privileges; do not give up your rights.' And they cried out in reply, 'No, never, never.' This comedy went on for days, so I heard, the jurymen standing their ground and Recorder Hywel maintaining that nothing would be right in England until they had the powers of the Spanish Inquisition to deal with such a rascal. In the end he fined the jurymen 40 marks apiece, and since they refused to pay, they were taken with the two prisoners to Newgate. But the jurymen were soon released and received recompense from the Recorder for wrongful arrest.

I wonder if Recorder Hywel is a Welshman? I have not heard either way but blush for his name. Dost thou know what G.F. himself said? He spoke of the opportunity he had in Newgate to propagate the Gospel of Light among the other prisoners. Not a word about his own all too obvious suffering —only gratitude to God for such a valuable opportunity. Listening to him I felt certain that there was a troubled time ahead of us. But, dear Margaret, we must make the most of adversity. Through our suffering others will find the solace of everlasting love. I know that God is strengthening us now for what is to come. We have not met in secret in the dark of night like the Presbyterians and the Baptists. Let them be judge of the rightness of that. For our part we must increase our witness and use our persecution to grind the mills of God.

My kindest regards to thee and to thy sister and to all Friends who meet at thy house.

From thy cousin,

Rowland Ellis.

He had hoped to have a word with Fox after the meeting but William Penn and his wife Guilielma had ushered him off to their own home. As he left the Meeting House, he saw three men speaking together, and brightened as he recognised them. He had not seen John ap John since he was a child but he had met the other two fairly often during his journeyings for the Quakers. Richard Davies and Thomas Lloyd, Dolobran, were Montgomeryshire men. The three turned to greet him, and John ap John said, 'Let us hear the opinion of a young man. We were speaking of New Jersey.'

'New Jersey?'

'Yes, in America. William Penn and two other men have a large piece of land there and propose to people it with men and women who wish to live in a country where there is freedom of conscience. Wouldst thou go there, Rowland Ellis?'

He laughed lightly. 'No, I would not.'

'Why not?' The question was shot at him by an unsmiling Thomas Lloyd.

'Well . . . for several reasons. My home is here. My family have farmed Bryn Mawr for almost a century. Why should I leave it? But apart from that, have we not a duty to remain here —to overcome whatever we may suffer?'

'What did I tell thee, Thomas Lloyd?'

Richard Davies turned to the other man. 'That was my feeling and I'm glad to have it confirmed by this young man. Leave America to the other Dissenters, I say. We have a mission and work to do in Wales.'

'But suppose the persecution becomes worse and frightens our people so much they do not own us. This has happened, remember, in other parts of the country. Would it not be better for us to go somewhere new to establish a completely free community. Imagine the effect on the rest of the world to see a fine, God-fearing country prosper because each man has the freedom to worship according to his conscience.'

'Utopia?'

'But it's possible.'

'No good ever came of running away.'

Rowland realised that John ap John was listening intently to the other two without offering an opinion of his own. He ventured once again, with a laugh.

'But surely this is an academic question. None of it is likely to arise for us. We are Welshmen, after all.'

'Not so academic,' said Thomas Lloyd. 'William Penn wants us to find settlers from among the Welsh . . . .It's obvious thou wilt not be among them, Rowland Ellis.'

Rowland smiled gently and shook his head.

On his way back to Wales the following week he pondered over this conversation. What if some of the Welsh Quakers were tempted to go? it would be very hard on the ones left behind. Would

Thomas Lloyd be among William Penn's first emigrants? He had not said he would, but he certainly seemed enthusiastic. Rowland found it all very hard to understand. There was Dolobran, a fine old manor house, and the Lloyds an honoured and respected family in the county. But one had to remember that Thomas had spent eight years of his life in Welshpool jail. Who could blame him for being attracted to the idea of peace and freedom in another country?

As for himself, he could not imagine living anywhere but at Bryn Mawr. And even if he had wanted to go, what would happen to the other Friends—those like Robert Ellis, Tyddyn-y-Garreg, Siân Morris and her father, Lewis Owen, Gwanas . . . ? These were the ordinary people of Wales, drawing their life's breath from the moorland peat and the craggy slopes of Cader Idris.

Margaret Owen, Dyffrydan what of her? And his own children, and Malan, and Ellis Puw? Even if he took them all with him, as one big family, how would those like Ellis Puw and Dorcas, speaking only Welsh, manage in the company of strangers of other nations, cut off from their roots? No, there was not the slightest chance that he would be lured by William Penn's plans.

He suddenly realised that he was annoyed with Penn for upsetting things, just when the people of Wales were beginning to be aware of the True Light.

Dorcas looked up at the restless clouds and quickened her pace. If she hurried it would take her a quarter of an hour to reach Bryn Mawr and maybe she would get there before the rain fell. It was getting dark, too, and the trees were swaying menacingly in the wind. All day the October sunshine had brightened the autumn leaves, warming the red fern on the banks behind the house so that her heart was filled with a happiness she wanted to share with Ellis. She had promised to meet him on Sunday—three nights to wait. Suddenly, after supper, she had decided to walk over to Bryn Mawr.

'But it's five o'clock already, night will fall before 'ee reach there,' warned Sinai, wondering at her prudent daughter's unusual impetuosity.

'I've cat eyes in the dark,' laughed Dorcas. 'And Ellis will bring me back long before midnight.'

But by now she was not so happy. The whine of the wind had turned into a doleful howl and she felt sure she could see a light shining in front of her as if from some ghostly jack-o-lantern. Her cheeks hurt as the strings from her woollen cap whipped across them in the wind and her skirts swirled round her legs, hampering her progress. The clouds were rolling like a pot on the boil and the first drop of rain touched her cheek as she turned towards the stream that ran into the river Aran, not far from Bryn Mawr. She was soaking by the time she reached the kitchen door.

Lisa stared at her, afraid some calamity had happened at home.

'No, there's nothing wrong. I'm sorry to have frightened 'ee. Where's Ellis?'

Lisa began to take off Dorcas's coat.

'Never mind Ellis. Take those wet clothes off and come to the fire.'

Dorcas shook her head and a shower of rainwater fell to the floor. 'I'll take off my stockings and dry my feet. The rest is all right.'

But Lisa was insistent.

'I'll bolt the door if thee be afraid someone'll come. Thee can wear my red dress while the clothes be dryin'.'

Seeing the state of her skirt and shawl beneath her cloak, Dorcas had no choice but to agree.

'Red dress? I didn't know 'ee had one.'

Lisa lowered her eyelids for a moment, then she said lightly: 'Oh, yes. I've had it a long time. Don't 'ee remember? It came from Jane Owen, Dolserau.'

It was a plain dress but it was the colour of strawberry juice and the fine, rich material fell in graceful folds from Dorcas's waist.

'Where's the fichu?' she asked, realising that the lowcut neck revealed too much of her bosom. Lisa was busy setting out the wet garments before the fire.

'There is no fichu.'

Dorcas blushed and crossed her hands in front of her breasts, looking anxiously through the window. She wanted to ask her

119

sister what occasion she had to wear such an immodest gown and she only a servant at Bryn Mawr. But she refrained for she was afraid to hear the answer.

'Are 'ee feeling more comfortable now? These clothes won't take a minute to dry before the fire, then I'll go and fetch Ellis for 'ee.'

Dorcas looked around her and saw that everything was neat and tidy, the stone floor almost white from constant scrubbing and the dresser and corner cupboard shining in the firelight.

'Is Malan better?'

'No, she's still abed. The doctor says her heart's weak after that last bout.'

'Lisa ran her hands over the steaming clothes and Dorcas saw her eyes in the firelight. They were glinting like frost in the sun.

'I'm not afraid of work,' and she added slowly, 'if I'm allowed to mind my own business.'

Dorcas was puzzled. Since Lisa had come to Bryn Mawr she had become something of a stranger to her sister. Of course, perhaps she was to blame too. Ellis filled so much of her life, she might have neglected Lisa. And yet, there was something . . . She changed the subject.

'Where are the children?'

Lisa was sitting on the floor hugging her knees. She stared thoughtfully at the fire.

'With Margaret Owen, Dyffrydan, thank goodness. At least, while the master's in London.'

'She's some kind of relative, isn't she?'

Lisa threw her head back and looked at Dorcas from the corner of her eye.

'She's likely to be a closer relative one day, for sure.'

'What dost 'ee mean?'

'She'll be mistress of Bryn Mawr before long.'

The notion was new to Dorcas. For a man to marry twice— was that good or bad? Even if the first wife were dead. What would happen when all three met in Heaven? Which one would Rowland Ellis be with? But the Bible said there would be no husbands and wives in Heaven. So it did not matter. Dorcas did not like that idea. She wanted to be with Ellis in this world and in the next. And if Ellis died first—she forced herself to think of such a possibility—she would never, never, never marry anyone else.

'Are 'ee sure?'

'No, of course I'm not sure. But there are signs. Who does Rowland Ellis write to from London and everywhere else he goes, for that matter? Where do the children go all the time? Mistress Owen wants to get to know them well to make herself indispensable and to make sure the children get to love her.'

'Lisa, don't talk like that.'

Lisa got up slowly. 'Why not? If I can see things clearly why should I keep quiet about it? Remember I don't blame Margaret Owen. The master of Bryn Mawr is young and handsome and he's money enough. And she's welcome to the children, I'd say, especially that Ann.'

Dorcas looked troubled. 'I don't like to hear 'ee talk so, making things sound so unpleasant—and—and bad.'

Dorcas longed for her clothes to be dry so that she could see Ellis—Ellis who was so innocent, so clean and gentle and unmalicious. Tears gathered at the back of her eyes but they did not flow. She had long since learned to check them.

Suddenly she felt two arms around her and her sister's warm cheek brushing against her own.

'Thee be right, Dorcas. I'm a wretch sometimes. And th'art so good. Thee little knows how good. We be very different from each other.'

The room seemed full of reconciliation as the two sisters sat silently, close together. But their peace was suddenly shattered by a hammering on the outer door of the kitchen.

'Oh, mercy, I've locked the door,' exclaimed Lisa. 'It must be Ellis wondering what on earth is going on.' She raised her voice. 'All right. All right. I'm coming.'

'No, Lisa,' screeched Dorcas faintly. 'This dress . . . '

'Oh, Ellis won't mind. I'll explain to him,' called Lisa over her shoulder as she made for the door.

Dorcas was so anxious to see Ellis, so terrified he might go away, but also horrified at the prospect of his seeing her in that dress, that she snatched up her cloak. She knew at once that it was still too wet to wear. Well, perhaps Ellis would understand. Dorcas folded her hands across her breasts again and looked towards the door expectantly. By this time Lisa had unbolted and opened it. But it was not Ellis who stood on the threshold.

They saw two strangers wearing uniform that indicated their office only too well. The girls were terrified at the sight of them but managed to keep quiet.

'Is there a man here named Ellis Puw?'

Dorcas was sure she had screamed but no sound came from her lips. Lisa clasped her sister's hand tightly and the scream dissolved into a sigh. Had the men noticed? Lisa was the first to recover.

'No. There's no one here of that name. May I ask, Sir, what your business is with him?'

'We are constables. Why were you so long unbolting the door?' The speaker pushed into the room past the two girls. His eyes were red in the firelight and his beard dripped with rainwater. The younger constable followed him. His pale face was beardless.

'Where are you hiding him?'

Lisa stood in front of the bearded constable to block his way.

'We're not hiding anyone. We have nothing to do with Ellis Puw. Anyway, what do you want him for?'

'We've a warrant against him for causing a disturbance outside the Parish Church.'

Dorcas emerged from the shadows behind Lisa. She was hurt by the accusation and also by her sister's denial.

'Ellis Puw never created a disturbance in his life.'

The constable looked at her, seeing her properly for the first time. His eyes roved slowly from her face, down her neck and came to rest on the white nakedness of her bosom. A cold smile touched his mouth.

'Ellis Puw means something to you, then. Come here!'

Dorcas remained where she was. The constable snatched his sword from its sheath and bawled, 'Come here!'

Dorcas moved slowly forward to stand in front of him.

'When did you last see Ellis Puw?'

Dorcas, to her own surprise, answered in a steady voice,

'Last Sabbath day.'

'Ah, the Sabbath. Did Ellis Puw go to the Parish Church to worship like every good Christian? Did he? Answer me?'

'All I know about Ellis Puw is that he's a Christian who loves Christ, the Saviour of Mankind.'

The constable looked again at the low cut bodice and the richness of the dress. The cold smile returned to his face. Then deliberately he turned back to Lisa.

'You. Show me where the menservants sleep. Shadrach, you guard the other girl and see that she doesn't move a step.'

Lisa was about to refuse but changed her mind. Without a word she went out to the yard, followed by the constable.

With all her might Dorcas prayed that Ellis would keep away. The rain beat against the window, the only sound in the kitchen. The constable kept his eyes on her like a cat watching a mouse. Although she strained her ears, she was unable to decide whether or not she could hear the sound of approaching footsteps. Her nerves were like harp strings strung too tightly. She felt thankful that they had allowed dusk to turn into night without lighting either lamp or candle, so that the only illumination came from the fire. She started to move towards the shadows behind the settle but the constable intervened.

'Come back to the middle of the floor.'

His hand reached for his sword. There was nothing for it but to obey him. She moved towards him but was almost unaware of him. Her thoughts were with Lisa and the constable in the stable loft where the menservants slept. Dafydd would have gone to bed some time ago, for sure. Tom had just gone home to his mother at Bwlchcoch. Ellis would certainly arrive sooner or later, in either the kitchen or the stable loft. Dorcas willed with all her might for the constable to tire of waiting and go home before he arrived.

A burning coal dropped out of the fire and Dorcas moved forward to put it back. The young constable thought she was about to escape and he seized her wrist.

'Stay where you are, whore!'

Dorcas was terrified. No one had ever called her that before. She thought he was going to strike her but instead he pulled her back to the centre of the room and released her arm as if it were a burning brand. Then slowly he wiped his hand on his knee. Dorcas saw that his lips were trembling and that the sweat stood out on his pale forehead.

'Why did 'ee call me that?' Dorcas's voice was hoarse.

'Because you deserve it.' His reply came in a whisper, and it frightened Dorcas more than any shouting could possibly do.

'That dress . . . only a whore would dare . . . '

Dorcas managed a faint smile and crossed her arms over her chest again.

'It's a borrowed dress. I got wet through coming here. These are my clothes.' She pointed to the steaming garments in front of the fire.

But the constable refused to take his eyes off her. He went on as if he had not heard her, his voice rising:

'Babylon the Great, the Mother of harlots and abomination of the earth . . . And I saw the woman drunken with the blood of the saints and with the blood of the martyrs of Jesus . . .

His sword was unsheathed now, its fine edge glistening terrifyingly near her throat.

'Oh, God,' prayed Dorcas, 'if this is my last moment let me die worthy of thee. Ellis—Ellis, where are 'ee?'

'Answer me!'

She closed her eyes and with all her strength prevented herself from stepping backwards. Let it be quick. Let me be brave. Let it happen now before I falter.

But nothing did happen. Dorcas opened her eyes and saw the young man had turned his back on her. She swallowed painfully as if she could still feel the sharp blade touching her neck, but she knew that the danger had passed—at least for the moment.

'Too shameless to be afraid. That's why you stand there so still. Beelzebub is your God and your lover. You knew he would save you. You thought to tempt me, didn't you? You thought I would forget my duty in my desire to touch your breasts. But God gave me the strength to cast you aside. And I conquered Satan and his handmaiden.'

To her surprise she heard tears in his voice. Immediately she forgot her fears for herself and even for Ellis for the moment. This lad standing before her had no power to harm her for all his uniform and his sword. This was a troubled man and she must console him. Very gently she placed her hand on his shoulder. His response was swift. He shook himself free and brandished his sword above her head at the same time retreating to the furthermost part of the room.

Where was Ellis? And why were Lisa and the other constable so long in returning? By now her own courage was evaporating and she felt very tired. She was cold and trembling but dared not sit down, although her gaoler was now like a ghost in the shadows.

The sound of a man's laughter was the last thing she had expected to hear that night but it came from the other side of the door, which was suddenly thrown open. The older constable strode in with Lisa following. Dorcas peered into the pitch blackness behind them but there was no sign of Ellis. For the first time in what seemed hours Dorcas felt herself relax.

The constable was in high spirits. He allowed Lisa to brush past and gave her bottom a cheerful pat as she went. Lisa smiled back at him.

'Ho, Shadrach! Looking after your prisoner? What's the matter, man? You look put out.'

The young man remained in his corner of the room, his lips mumbling. The other man shrugged his shoulders and turned to Lisa.

'He gets bouts like this. But we've learnt not to take any notice. He does his work well enough.'

At this Shadrach emerged from the shadows, his fiery eyes turned on his superior. 'We came here with a warrant to arrest Ellis Puw.'

The other laughed. 'Right enough. Right enough, Shadrach.' He strode to the door once more.

'Well, if the bird isn't here there's no point in waiting, is there? We'll come back again.' He looked at Lisa and winked meaningly. 'And again . . . won't we, Shadrach?'

The two men regarded each other. the younger with fury in his eyes. His companion bellowed, 'Come on, Shadrach!'

They continued to eye each other with hostility, but Shadrach was the first to look away.

When the door had closed behind the two men, the girls heard peals of laughter ringing through the darkness. Dorcas shuddered. She felt Lisa's gaze on her but she did not return it. Her own emotions were in a turmoil. Relief that Ellis had escaped trouble, at least for the moment, surprise that the constable should have given in so easily, cold doubt about his reasons insinuating itself into her mind, and, throughout everything, the memory of Shadrach's venom and his misery. She stared into the fire.

Lisa thought; she's blaming me. But she should be grateful. The constables have gone, haven't they? And Ellis safe, for the time being, at any rate. If she loves Ellis it's worth any price. I did it for her and for Ellis—and there's no need for her to look like that. Why doesn't she say something? What's she thinking? That man might have wanted Dorcas and that would have been far worse. But it was me he wanted, so he said. Old hands needed old hands and let the young lads have the virgins. Those were his words, in spite of that dress Dorcas was wearing. And this is only the beginning of the payment, Dorcas, dost 'ee understand? He will be back again . . . *Will* he be back?

When Ellis returned about an hour later, having been to Brithdir in the hope of seeing Dorcas and disappointed at having missed her, Lisa had gone to bed, and Dorcas was still sitting there staring into the fire. He was dismayed at her pallor and the dark rings under her eyes. She gave a deep sigh of relief when she saw him and, laying her head on his breast, clutched him to her as if she would never let him go.

4

Rowland Ellis returned from London before the end of the week to discover that his youngest servant was in jail.

When Dorcas tried painfully and tearfully to explain to Ellis what had happened that night she did not mention the fears she had about her sister's behaviour. But Ellis Puw was no longer the innocent who had first come to Bryn Mawr. He understood immediately the reason for the constable's willingness to leave his work undone that night.

It was too high a price to pay for his freedom. Next evening he went down into the town and knocked at the door of Plas-yn-dre where Justice Lefi Huws lived. He denied the charge that he had created a breach of the peace outside the parish church, but he expected no mercy and received none. For the first time in his life he heard the gates of a prison close behind him.

Rowland went at once to try to see Ellis, taking Dorcas with him. A bribe to Siôn Prys let them in to the prison. They found him lying on a bed of dirty, smelly straw, but he did not complain. He hoped, he said, to be released before the end of February after he had stood trial at the old Courthouse.

Rowland did not know what to say to him. He could have bribed the guard still further to make sure that Ellis got special treatment but Rowland knew that Ellis would not want this. He was not the only Quaker in jail.

Rowland was appalled at the sordid surroundings: the lack of light—just a glimmer filtering through the iron bars in a hole in the wall—the filthy floor, the offensive smells and the shouts and moans of the other prisoners, each in a stall not fit for an animal, let alone a man. He looked at Ellis again and admired his gentle serenity and marvelled at the peace that possessed not only him but Dorcas as well.

Dorcas was used to hiding her feelings. But her tranquillity this time was not a camouflage or an escape. The agony when she had realised that Ellis was going to give himself up had become a kind of purification. The burden of guilt she had carried was lifted. She was prepared to accept anything now that Ellis had atoned for what had happened that night. Her gladness reached Ellis and comforted him.

Without understanding the reason for it, Rowland sensed the feelings that flowed between these two. Fervently he hoped that when his time came he would be able to face up to his trial with their dignity, for now he knew that it was merely a matter of time. He had already been warned that he was liable to be fined for not paying his tithes. He would still refuse to pay and the punishment would be imprisonment. In the meantime his duty was to see that Ellis Puw had a fair hearing.

On leaving gaol, he called on Lefi Huws. He came straight to the point.

'I would like to know, Lefi Huws, on what grounds my friend, Ellis Puw, has been imprisoned?'

The Justice was a small man. Whether his legs were bandy from constant riding to hounds or from birth it was hard to tell since his childhood was a long way behind him. That day he was suffering from a heavy cold and when Rowland was shown into the parlour he found the Justice in front of a mountainous fire, his feet submerged in a mustard bath. His wig stood idly on a table and on his head he wore a woollen nightcap.

Giving no sign of having heard his servant announce his visitor, nor of having heard Rowland's words, he continued to sneeze noisily into his handkerchief. Rowland waited patiently. When the noise stopped Rowland repeated his message. Lefi had now had time to collect his thoughts.

'On this warrant here it says Ellis Puw, servant of Rowland Ellis, gentleman. No mention of friend.'

'Ellis is a worker at Bryn Mawr, Lefi Huws. That is no hinddrance to his being my friend.'

'If your servant is in jail then he has committed an offence.'

Lefi emphasised the word 'servant' and suddenly looked sharply at Rowland.

'Sir, you are committing an offence at this moment.'

'So . . . ?'

'Your hat, sir. You dare to keep your hat on your head when you visit a gentleman in his house?'

Rowland replied courteously that it was not his habit to remove his hat as a mark of politeness. His respect for his host went deeper than mere gesture.

The Justice suffered another fit of coughing.

'Tis little wonder we imprison you Quakers,' he remarked between spasms. 'I've never heard such impudence.'

Having regained his breath, he went on with the shadow of a smile in his beady eyes, 'If everyone behaved in that fashion, there would be neither master, nor servant, authority nor respect. There would be chaos in the land. What say you to that, sir, hey?'

'No. For there's no place for chaos where love and truth are the rulers.'

'Brave words, young man. But when you have lived as long as I have you will realise that to few men are given love and truth. As a good Calvinist I would maintain these are given to only the chosen elect. Through the Fall. The rest of mankind is possessed by evil, vanity and deceit.'

'But every man has the Light if he will only listen to its message.'

Lefi Huws had dried his feet and was warming them in front of the fire. Rowland looked at him anew. He had not expected the Justice to enter into a discussion with him in this way.

'How can you be sure?' asked Lefi Huws, after a short silence. 'No—!' as Rowland attempted to reply. 'Allow me to ask you one question, sir. This Inner Light—oh, do not he surprised—I've read and listened. How can you be sure that the voice you hear is that of God and not of the Devil? Y'know, men can deceive themselves oddly, even good men. The voice of conscience and the voice of desire are often bedmates. And who am I, or who are you, to say that your conscience is right and mine not?'

'Because man's conscience is not the Light,' answered Rowland quietly. 'It is a gift from God. Morgan Llwyd said— "There is need for neither Bible nor preacher. The true preacher stands in the pulpit of our hearts and the Book within us will serve us if we follow it and take notice of it as the Word or a Candle burning within us in a dark place. We should obey the voice and follow the light within us."'

Lefi Huws threw back his head and guffawed.

'But Morgan Llwyd was a good Puritan, my boy. After all, he did not join your sect. Why? Because you go to ridiculous extremes.' He turned his head and his voice was almost friendly. 'Tell me, why must you and your sort be such a nuisance to us?'

He got up slowly and came towards Rowland placing his hand on his shoulder.

'Listen, my boy. Believe what you wish but don't make an exhibition of it. Go to Church on Sundays, pay your tithes and do nothing likely to divide the country more than it is divided already. No one can take your creed away from you but for the sake of peace and common sense keep quiet about it.'

Rowland shook his head slowly.

'I know thy intentions are good, Lefi Huws.' The Justice winced at the too familiar 'thy'. 'But for me, to work that way would deprive my life of meaning.' He turned towards the Justice, deeply moved. 'Canst thou not see that I must act according to the Light of Christ? I have no choice.'

The Justice's face hardened.

'There is no luxury greater than that of self-righteousness. If my conscience is satisfied, then the Church, the country, the King and the law can all go to the devil. That's what your words imply. But you are too young yet to realise how offensive this is. And now, with your permission, I will finish dressing.'

He turned his back on Rowland.

'And Ellis Puw' asked the young man.

'His trial will be a fair one.'

Rowland stared at the stiff back and realised there was no point in further discussion. He pulled his hat more firmly on his head.

'Peace be with thee,' he said and left.

Ellis was duly brought to trial but was in court barely ten minutes. He was offered a Bible and commanded to raise his right hand to take the oath of abjuration. Ellis refused, explaining carefully that his conscience did not allow him to take such an oath.

'Take him away,' ordered Lefi Huws coldly.

Each of the Quakers, seven of them in all, was treated in the same way, either for contempt of court in refusing to take off their hats or for refusing to take the oath.

Rowland glanced at Dorcas. She was pale but composed. A little of her tranquillity reached him and consoled him. Before leaving the court he asked for writing paper, a quill and ink. Addressing a note to Lefi Huws, he handed it to one of the constables. A messenger brought the brief reply– 'No'.

Rowland was aware that all the known Quakers in the neighbourhood would be sent to join Ellis Puw and the others as soon as plausible excuses could be found. In fact, he was surprised that he himself had escaped for so long. Once again he felt a deep concern, not for what might happen to him, but for the future of his children. It was obvious that Malan was too old to cope with them. Lisa? Above all the two little girls needed someone to teach them the difference between right and wrong.

Only one person could do this to his satisfaction. The step by step of his reasoning was familiar to him by now. Night after night he would lie awake in bed questioning himself. Should he ask Marged Owen, Dyffrydan, to marry him? The children loved her, and she loved them. She understood and shared his deepest spiritual longings. So it would be no sacrifice for her to face the dangers of being the wife of a Quaker. He would have peace of mind (if the justices gave him freedom) to journey about the country preaching. He knew she was a good housewife and Bryn Mawr would be a more orderly place than it had been since his mother's time.

What then hindered him? Every time he arrived at this stage in his thoughts, his imagination painted pictures which blotted out all his careful reasoning. He would see a cloud of silken hair floating over the pillow, a neck as smooth as a dove melting into two warm breasts and a cool thigh lying outside the bedclothes waiting for him to cover it with his body.

He told himself that death strengthened romantic memories and drew a veil over the bad. Huw Morris's last malicious words still rang in his ears. But another part of him clamoured, 'I am twenty-six years old and love and passion are still within me.' Oh, he admired Marged Owen for her gentleness, for her sweet composure and understanding. His mind ran swiftly over her virtues — he admired her in the same way as he admired Ellis Puw and Jane Owen. But surely something more was needed if he was to share his bed with a woman for a lifetime? He was no nearer to knowing the answer.

Lefi Huws was thoughtful. Did Rowland Ellis really expect him to take his suggestion seriously? If not, then this offer to take Ellis Puw's place in jail was pretence and hypocrisy of the first order. If he meant it, well, offers like this had been made by Quakers before, so he had heard. In fact, it was known that such self-sacrifice had earned the admiration of Cromwell himself a quarter of a century earlier. Lefi also knew that Rowland Ellis constantly visited his Quaker friends in Dolgellau gaol and was therefore not unaware of conditions inside those walls.

Damnation take these people! So convinced they knew the ways of God better than anyone else. Some of them were quite harm-less, basically — Tomos Ellis, the genial farmer from Iscregennan and the Gwanas brothers. But obstinate! Heavens, how obstinate they were. Well, it was not he who was responsible for formulat-ing the laws. He merely administered them. The bloody years of war and disorder had given him enough regard for law and order to insist that the laws of the land must be respected.

Lefi Huws had been a young officer in Maesygarnedd's army and memories of the atrocities of the '40's still haunted him. He could still hear the screams of violated women and children, could see the stockyards burn and the bodies of men he had known rotting in the streets. Man against his brother, treachery, corruption and revenge. Was it any wonder that he worshipped now at the altar of law and order? The law was the only hope for the survival of civilisation. Mercy was a dangerous weakness. When Maesygarnedd was executed in '60, Lefi pledged himself to the new King and swore to uphold authority at all times.

He had fallen out with his cousin, Robert Owen, for taking the opposite view. But Robert had always been a rebel. Well, some people derived a curious pleasure out of self-punishment, like Roman monks flagellating themselves with sticks. The Quakers were just as bad, welcoming imprisonment as an opportunity to spread their gospel inside the jail, or so they said.

If Rowland Ellis persisted in this stupidity, he must take the consequences. He yawned, stretched his arms above his head, and went upstairs to his bedroom, where the servant had just removed the warming pan from his master's bed.

Early next morning he received a visit which caused him some surprise since he knew it to be the habit of the Reverend Morris Jones to sleep until mid-day—to sleep, in fact, until he had sobered up, thought Lefi Huws.

But today, for once, there seemed to be no sign of the previous night's drinking. The reverend gentleman walked carefully into the parlour, ceremoniously holding out his hand. His mouth is as small as a cockerel's arse, thought Lefi, for there was little love lost between the two men. Taking a drop was one thing, but to see any man, let alone a parson, reeling about offended the orderly Lefi's ideas of propriety. And that was how he saw Morris Jones more often than not.

'Your servant, Sir,' said Lefi, inclining his head as little as politeness demanded.

'Forgive me for disturbing you so early and you—' began the parson, his voice syrupy.

Lefi interrupted him impatiently.

'Your message must be very important.'

'Well, yes, it is. Or I would not dream of taking up your time.'

'Yes?'

'Well, of course, you will realise that I must take heed of everything I hear in these troubled times, *cum grano salis*, of course. Would you not agree? But all the same . . . '

Lefi looked pointedly at the big clock in the corner. Not even the parson could ignore the hint. The syrup disappeared from his voice.

'Things came to my hearing last night, such things that drove sleep entirely away.'

Liar, thought Lefi Huws, there's nothing would disturb your drunken sleep. But he kept his reflections to himself.

'Who, in your opinion, is the most dangerous man in our midst today?'

Lefi Huws opened his snuff box and offered it to the parson, noticing that the latter's hand was trembling as he lifted the snuff to his nostrils.

'The Devil, I should say.'

'Yes, yes, but in which people does the Devil dwell, would you say?'

Lefi answered lightly. 'I—you, sir. In me. In him. In every human creature.'

'Would you not say that Rome is the abode of Satan?'

Lefi regarded his visitor with curiosity. 'Well?'

'And that the Papists lurk secretly under other names?'

The Reverend Morris Jones leaned forward in his chair with excitement.

'I have a witness prepared to swear he has seen a cross and altar in a secret room in a farmhouse not far from this town. Furthermore, he has seen men kneel and say prayers before a statue of the Virgin Mary.'

'Who is this witness?'

'A man by the name of Huw Morris—'

Lefi Huws interrupted him with a laugh.

'I had an idea it might be someone like that. I venture, too, to name the farm. Bryn Mawr, hey? Upon my soul, sir, the ramblings of a vindictive ex-servant would hardly be likely to keep me awake o'nights.'

The parson was furious. But Lefi Huws was a man of some weight in the community and the syrup returned to his voice.

'It's possible you are right. Although I've enough experience of Papist cunning to be surprised at nothing. You must agree that they continue to be a danger to the very existence of the State. You will also agree, no doubt, that they have wondrous influence in high places?'

'You are referring to His Majesty, King Charles, of course,' barked Lefi Huws.

The parson pursed his lips and looked hurriedly over his shoulder.

'I did not say that.' His voice was no more than a whisper. 'All I'm suggesting is that we must take serious note of every accusation until it be proved baseless.'

'If I listened to all the tittle-tattle that comes to my ears I would be hearing cases night and day. What do you want of me, man? To put Rowland Ellis in irons because his servant wants his revenge?'

The parson rose to his feet, his head trembling uncontrollably.

'If you are not prepared to listen to Huw Morris's evidence perhaps you will listen to mine. I heard the master of Bryn Mawr addressing a crowd of people on the Church common. He blasphemed against God's Church and its ministers. I heard him with my own ears uttering the most wicked slander against me personally. And he had the hold of the Devil over the people. I had to suffer hearing them mock me. I, the servant of God. Lefi Huws, I demand that this dangerous man be punished.'

'On the grounds of slander against you—or on the grounds of being a Papist?'

'On the grounds of being a wicked blasphemer. His tongue should be torn out and his forehead branded.'

In the silence that followed, the head of the Justice fell lower and lower on his chest. The parson thought he had fallen asleep. But suddenly Lefi Huws got up, walked to the window, then turned sharply and stood there, his fat legs apart.

'You know, and I know, sir, that Huw Morris is a coward and a shameless informer. But we will forget that for the moment. Once and for all we must restore order to this community. We are both agreed that the Law and the Church are the foundations of a secure Protestantism.'

'Indeed .'

'Therefore, we must strengthen the arm of the Church. If we have been too slack with backsliders, it is we who must pay the

135

penalty in the long run. Let me have the names of those absent from worship at the Parish Church during the next month and I will see that they come before court.'

The two men glared at each other like two cockerels before a fight. A thin smile spread across the parson's lips.

There was a smile also on Huw Morris's lips as he stood in the shelter of the yew tree while a sharp March wind whipped up the straw and dust from the rutted wayside. A bell hanging from the yew tree rang as if shaken by a madman. From here he could see the market stalls, the women selling their butter and eggs and the men their early lambs and piglets.

Lisa was carrying a heavy basket and weaving her way through the noisy crowd. In a moment he was at her side, relieving her of the burden of the basket.

'It's too heavy for'ee, little one.'

She turned on him sharply. 'I'll neither be looking for nor expecting politeness from 'ee, Huw Morris.'

'Don't be unkind. I'm tha friend.'

She had become thinner. Her face was paler and the features more defined but her lips were soft and ripe. And this new coldness in her eyes was a challenge.

'I've got something to tell 'ee.'

'It's no use.'

They had to jump out of the way of a horse-and-cart bowling along through the crowd which pressed in on them, giving Huw the chance to put his arm round Lisa's waist. He felt the shiver than ran through her body at his touch and, like a hawk, he saw how her eyes half-closed and her lips parted.

'Come to Pandy Woods,' he whispered in her ear. 'There's a warm barn on the way.'

After all, he was fond of the girl. Limp as a rag doll when he touched her yet tart enough of tongue to give relish to the game. It occurred to him that it might be a good idea to keep her away from Bryn Mawr tonight, in any case.

'Hywel Vaughan took me in after I left Bryn Mawr, did 'ee know?'

Lisa pushed on, ignoring him, but it was impossible to make much progress through the surging crowd ahead of her with Huw clinging firmly to her arm.

'That's a real place is Hengwrt. Even the maids sleep under silken sheets.'

Lisa knew that Huw was lying but her curiosity had been aroused. He saw that she was listening intently.

'And the gentry from London—'ee never did see the like. Dancing and playing dice until cockcrow. The energy of these people! They're out before noon hunting the stag or the hare. And ye'd be 'mazed when they come out to see their husbands off. Listen, I must tell 'ee this, and 'ee'll laugh. One time I got a crown piece from one of 'em. A penny most of 'em give, 'ee know. When she'd given me the crown she asked me to go to the stable in a quarter of an hour's time to see to her horse . Can 'ee guess why? There was no one else around when her ladyship came there—to get her full crown's worth.'

A stab of jealousy shot through Lisa. She turned her head away.

'I'll not be listening to any more of tha lies, Huw Morris. Let me go.'

He laughed. 'I could tell 'ee a lot more, my girl. But there 'tis. If 'ee don't want to hear, that's it, isn't it?'

'I didn't intend to hurt tha feelings, Huw. I'm glad th'art happy in tha new place. Truly I am.'

Huw drew her hand through his arm.

'Well, come somewhere warmer to listen to me then.'

He took her basket and they both started off through Penucha'r-dre towards Pandy Woods.

Why was the door open? She had expected to see a lamp in at least one of the windows. It must be later than she thought. But why was the door open?

She stood on the threshold, rigid. The silence was unbearable.

'Master!'

Only the wind replied with an echo, and everywhere it was as dark as the tomb. Disaster had struck the world and only she was left.

'Master!'

A cry rose in her throat. She looked towards the stable loft but there was no glimmer from there either. Everywhere was dead. I am the only one left. Oh, Mam fach, what shall I do? Oh, God, don't punish me like this. I'll never do it again. Only let me know that this is a bad dream and that I'll wake up soon.

Dorcas. Dorcas was coming to the meeting tonight. And Lewis Owen, Tyddyn-y-Garreg. And Dafydd Ifan from Llanfachreth with Gainor, his wife, and others she couldn't remember now. Where was everyone? Perhaps the master had seen some of them home by lamplight. But Dorcas? Dorcas had said she would wait for her. And Malan? What about Malan? And the children?

She could stand the suspense no longer. Running wildly into the house she called out; 'Malan! Malan!'

From upstairs there was a sound of a child crying, then another joined in. Lisa rushed upstairs, weeping tears of relief to know that at least the two children were alive.

'Ann! Ann! What's the matter? Where are you?'

Hearing her, the two little girls howled without restraint.

'Want a light! Want a light!' Ann was shouting.

'All right, little one. Lisa's coming now.'

She ran downstairs again as fast as the darkness allowed, to look for a candle. Finding one at last, she lit it from the embers of the dying fire. She almost fainted when she saw the disorder all around her; upturned chairs scattered over the floor, more chairs than she had ever seen there before. The meeting, of course !

The dresser was empty of its pewter pots, porridge had been spilled over the oak settle by the fireside, and the open window swung madly backwards and forwards on its hinges. She ran upstairs again trying to call words of comfort to the children. Ann kept on crying, but Siân stood in her nightdress twisting a lock of hair around her finger, her mouth wide open and a faraway, foolish look in her eyes.

'Malan s'eeping.'

Lisa caught Ann to her and hugged the small, trembling body.

'There 'ee are, my lovely. 'Ee'll be all right now.'

'Malan s'eeping.'

Siân was too young to understand fear and she wasn't all there in any case. Ann was the one who needed comforting. What had the little one seen? The younger child started to laugh hysterically.

'Stop making that silly noise, Siân, and go back to bed.'

Between Ann's sobbing and Siân's laughter, Lisa did not know what to do.

'What happened? Where's everyone? Tell Lisa. No, don't cry any more. Tell me quietly.'

At last the words came through the tears. Big strong men had come and made a noise all over the house. They had been locked in the room by one of the men. There had been a terrible noise and one of the men had hair on his hands and he had turned himself into a weasel and jumped on Malan.

'Malan!' shrieked Siân, hearing the name. 'Malan s'eeping.'

A sudden fear seized Lisa. She raised the candle above her head and looked around her.

'Where is Malan, Ann?'

Ann clutched at Lisa's skirt tightly and hid her face in its folds, whimpering once again. But Siân took her finger out of her mouth and pointed towards the darkest recesses of the room.

'Malan s'eeping. Malan s'eeping on the floor over there.'

Slowly Lisa approached the bundle of clothes on the floor. Fearfully she turned the garments over. Then she started to moan softly.

'Oh God! Oh God!'

She was still there when Marged Owen arrived to take the children into her care.

5

Dolgellau gaol had never been so full. The rector had kept a careful record of the names of all those who had not attended St. Mary's Church for a whole month. The result was an amazing conglomeration of backsliders, with almost half the population behind bars, men and women alike. As well as the Quakers there were Baptists, Independents, Socinians, Antinomians and followers of various other sects, and the plain lazy.

But after a week or two the numbers became fewer and fewer. The reason for this was not hard to find. When the prisoners were brought to trial the justices required everyone to swear an oath of allegiance to King and State. They all obeyed —except the Quakers. They, twenty nine in all, stood there each in turn reciting:

'Christ our Lord saith,"Swear not at all, neither by heaven for it is God's throne; nor by the earth; for it is his footstool: neither by Jerusalem; for it is the city of the great king. Neither shalt thou swear by thy head because thou canst not make one hair white or black. But let your communication be yea, yea, and nay, nay; for whatsoever is more than these cometh of evil."'

Everyone in court knew what the outcome would be. It had all happened before to people like Robert Owen, Dolserau, and Cadwaladr Tomos from Bala. The Quakers would be fined fifty pounds each. They would refuse to pay, whereupon their land would be confiscated and auctioned by the sheriff. A man without any means would be imprisoned.

Rowland was thankful that Marged Owen was free. He knew she would take care of the children. Lewis Owen, Tyddyn-y-Garreg, had promised to look after the farm but Lewis's own future was uncertain, since he and his family had now joined the Friends.

Lisa flatly refused to leave Bryn Mawr. For some reason she felt responsible for Malan's death and Marged had been unable to comfort her. So Marged had decided to stay on at Bryn Mawr with Lisa and the children until Rowland returned. Old Dafydd could hardly be expected to take charge of everything but he would do his best, and Twm would come over from Bwlch-coch every day to help out.

But as it happened there was no need to worry. One morning the jailer opened the door, unfolded a scroll and read out a list of names.

"Free to go forth, by the grace of His Majesty: Rhisiart Humphrey, Elis Morus, Lewis Ifan, Rowland Ellis . . ."

Rowland inquired why Ellis Puw and Dorcas were not included but the jailer refused to answer. Rowland Ellis insisted, as a free citizen, on seeing Lefi Huws.

'The reason is a simple one,' said the Justice. 'When you reach home you will find that you have fifty pounds' worth of stock less than you had before. As far as I know neither Ellis Puw nor Dorcas Robarts has fifty pounds, so they must remain where they are. Such is the law of the land.'

'Send thy servants to fetch another hundred pounds' worth of my stock, said Rowland. 'I cannot go free and leave behind those who are in my care.'

He was longing to see the children and to smell again the scent of the earth around Bryn Mawr. As Ellis, Dorcas and he climbed the slopes to freedom once again, he was surprised to realise how depressed he felt. Around him the buds of hazel and rowan shone a deep green after the rain. Primroses and celandines formed yellow carpets on the banks. Thrush and blackbird vied in song and the clouds raced smoothly in the free sky. But all this only underlined his gloom.

> Oh my heart, break if thou must
> Take away my timeless hope
> Breaking slowly, piece by piece,
> Like blue ice on glassy slope.

Curious how one remembered the old verses at such a time. This was only the beginning. He knew the losses Robert Owen,

Dolserau, had suffered over the years. What if they kept on putting him in prison until he found one day that Bryn Mawr had all been taken from him? Although the sun was still shining, he realised he was shivering.

Ellis and Dorcas were walking hand in hand a few steps behind him, their faces a reproach to his depression. He almost envied them for having no possessions to fetter their faith in the glorious present. And yet flesh itself was a fetter. He remembered the words of the Dove: 'Flesh is everything under the sun that is exterior to the inner man. Whatsoever is finite and is not eternal is of the flesh. All man's senses and worldly pleasures they are of flesh. Flesh is the gaiety of young and old. Flesh is time and all that comes to an end with it. Flesh is the will and mystery of man. Flesh is much praying and preaching. And all flesh is straw. This flesh is the enemy of God, the poison of man, the livery of hell . . . '

He heard the two of them laugh as Ellis lifted Dorcas over a marshy patch of ground. They had already forgotten the iron doors of the prison.

As he had expected, Marged Owen and Lewis Tyddyn-y-Garreg were there to welcome them. But his first concern was for the children. The sound of their screaming from upstairs that night while he had to stand by helpless in the hands of the soldiers still echoed in his ears. They were shy and hid behind Marged, but she led them gently towards him. Rowland hugged them to him tightly as tears gathered in his eyes.

Lewis told him how the Sheriff's men had taken some of the best cattle and had then returned to seize a further lot so that Ellis and Dorcas could be released.

'A loss of about five hundred pounds for thee, I'd say. But, if thou wilt let me I would like to give thee some of my stock, to lessen thy loss a little. Repay me later as thou wilt.'

Rowland Ellis was surprised. Although Lewis was not exactly a miser, Rowland knew that he counted his pence carefully. If ever there was clear evidence of the change of heart that came with knowledge of the Inner Light, then here it was in Lewis Owen's offer.

That night, after holding a Meeting at Bryn Mawr, Rowland Ellis asked Marged Owen to marry him and she accepted.

The sun shines briefly in the Mawddach Valley but when it does everywhere is transfigured. The deep shadows cast by the trees seem deeper against the brilliance of the meadow. How beautiful the green looks against the blue of the sky, reflected Dorcas, as she gazed up at the tapestry of leaves. By the time they had turned to red and gold she would be Ellis's wife. She lifted her skirts a little and started to run, jumping from one mound to the other, until she remembered the eggs in her basket.

In ten minutes I shall be in the town and within an hour I shall have sold all the eggs and be on the way to Bryn Mawr and him. Ellis, Ellis, Ellis . . .

Her lips shaped his name over and over playfully, then tenderly, now with a deep and sensuous sigh, now in the sort of way her mother would say her name.

And yet a lump came to her throat because sadness was so near to great happiness. She tried to concentrate on the autumn and imagine what her life would be like as Ellis Puw's wife. Rowland Ellis had promised them a small cottage on the edge of his land. She and Ellis had been to see it. It was a tiny two-roomed cottage but so cosy, with real windows instead of shutters. If they could be left in peace until the autumn, life would be paradise indeed.

Marged Owen and Rowland Ellis would be marrying about the same time and her heart warmed at the thought. Marged was quiet but comforting to be with. Dorcas particularly liked her smile, not a false, empty, forced smile but a smile that appeared in the eyes before reaching the lips, as the little wrinkles at the corners well showed.

She was the only one who could control the children. Ann was lively and very pretty. 'Miss Mischief' everyone called her, but affectionately. Siân was different, with her lank hair and dribble, her frenzied screaming, and her humming for hours on end. It was only with Marged that she was perfectly quiet. She would climb on to her knee and resting her head on Marged's breast, would be lulled into drowsiness by the rise and fall of Marged's breathing.

Like everyone else, Dorcas had heard about Siân's mother and the manner in which the second child had been born. Lisa had often recounted her own version of what had happened, what she knew, or what she imagined had happened. Did Marged Owen know? Surely they would not keep secrets from each other. Certainly she would tell Ellis everything about herself and he would keep nothing from her. And back her thoughts inevitably turned to Ellis again.

The town wore a fresh, new look; the old stones were dried out clean after the May showers but not yet swept by the hazy dust of summer. She passed a group of children playing at dancing around a maypole, which was in fact a branch of white-thorn. Faster and faster they ran around the little girl who held the branch until they stumbled, falling in a heap on top of one another. From the bottom of the heap came the smothered cries of the little May Queen.

Fun had turned to fear. Dorcas ran towards the children, but no one was hurt so she went on her way. A few yards away from where the children played was a bridge. But as she was about to cross it, someone stepped in front of her like a black cloud covering the sun. She felt suddenly cold as she recognised the thin, pale face of Shadrach the constable. He said nothing but his eyes were like the tips of two unsheathed swords. She tried to push past him but he took a step to the left to stop her.

It dawned on Dorcas that the man was mad. Petrified, she looked around for help. Behind her the children were once again absorbed in their game. In front of her three women were beginning to raise their voices in argument; boys were fishing lazily at the water's edge; two old men sat silently nearby wrapped in their own thoughts and there was no one else in sight. Shadrach was beginning to speak.

'What did you do to the children, you witch? What spell did you cast on them, eh?' Between every audible phrase his lips kept on working.

'She was like you . . . every whore's the same.'

Although it was broad daylight and although there were people around, Dorcas was more afraid of him this time than during their last encounter at Bryn Mawr. She could barely hear what he was saying, so low was his voice.

'She had the same hair, the same mouth . . . and she liked showing her breasts for the world to see . . . The men would come, one after the other, leaving a crown on the table, one, two, three . . . ' His voice rose in a sob.

'So that I had to cover my ears with the bedclothes to shut out the sound of their footsteps. A crown . . . a crown, did 'ee hear? A crown. And her own crown smashed to tiny pieces on the floor like trampled glass.'

She turned to escape, but he held her tightly by the wrist.

'A crown I said. And the little fool calling for his mother while she gave her full breasts to men, one after the other. You, too, you witch.'

He was twisting her arm and Dorcas began to call for help. The women ceased their quarrelling, the boys looked up from their fishing and a frightened hush fell on the children. Only the two old men continued to gaze unheedingly into the distance. They had seen it all before.

One of the women shouted and Dorcas felt Shadrach's grip on her weaken for a moment. She tore herself away from him and ran with all her strength towards the town where she hoped to escape into the thronged market. She could hear someone giving chase but dared not turn round to see whether or not it was Shadrach. She ran until the blood sang in her ears and her legs felt numb. She was now outside the Golden Lion yard, horses and carts passing her by, and began to think her danger over when she saw him coming round the corner from the direction of Owen Glyndwr's old Parliament House, a mob of people behind him shouting and waving sticks.

'To the Red Chair with her!'

'To the river with the witch!'

'She's a Quaker. I saw her in court.'

This was proof of her guilt. But what need was there of proof? Shadrach was a constable, so this time it would be safe enough to have some sport. If the girl wasn't a witch, she was a blaspheming

Quaker and deserved her punishment. If she was a witch, then they had to protect their children, their husbands, their herds.

The jeering faces were now bearing down upon her, surrounding her, pulling her cap from her head and throwing it in the air. She could feel feverish fingers clawing at her throat and ripping her dress to shreds.

She raised her head as she heard the word 'Quaker'. Immediately her fears dissolved. Someone was at her side holding her hand, sustaining her. She turned to him, tears of relief streaming down her cheeks.

'Father!'

But there was no warm, familiar face near her, only harsh guffaws and mocking voices crying, 'How! Come on! How! How!'

Sticks slashed down on her bare back as she was driven towards the bottom of the bridge. Excitement throbbed through the crowd, in anticipation of what lay ahead. No one had been in the Red Chair since the time of Betsan Prys and rumour had it that the law was going to clamp down on the ancient practice of ducking witches. Before long there would be no fun in seeing that justice was done, and the law would allow every witch to do her work. Well, it was not the law yet, and if they got rid of a witch who was known to be a sour-faced, blaspheming Quaker to boot, why, so much the better.

The Red Chair was brought forward, an old iron contraption, rusty through many duckings in the river Wnion. Dorcas was pushed into it and the crossbar clicked into place.

Shadrach and another man with legs long enough to stand comfortably in the deep water held each side of the chair firmly.

'One . . . two . . . three.' The shout rang out, but she did not hear it. She was sailing through the air, her inside rising against it. Then she was fighting for breath as the water filled her ears, eyes and mouth.

'Up with her, boys. Now then. Once again. One . . . two . . . three.'

By the third ducking she had lost consciousness.

Gwallter, the thatcher, from Ganllwyd, had been watching it all with alarm and compassion. It was not the first time he had seen a woman ducked in the Red Chair. In the old days it had happened often, too often to arouse any feelings of concern. But since the Protectorate it had not happened so often. Perhaps official disapproval was giving an edge to the cruelty of the mob today. Perhaps more primitive emotions were being aroused in the men at the sight of a pretty girl rather than an old crone. Gwallter did not rightly know but he did know that it had all been as sickening to him as if someone had given him a punch in the stomach. Shadrach was yelling at the other man to keep tight hold of the chair ready for another ducking but he, looking down at the helpless girl, suddenly mumbled. 'No, no . . . That's enough.'

The crowd agreed. Having had their fun, they were beginning to feel uneasy and looked at Shadrach as people do at a man who is still drunk when the rest have sobered up. One by one they stole away until only Shadrach was left with a handful of bystanders and Gwallter.

Shadrach gave the girl's saturated body a jerk, mumbling, 'Mam . . . mam . . . mam.'

'Leave her alone now, friend,' said Gwallter, placing his hand on the young constable's shoulder. Shadrach shook himself like a dog come out of the water, then suddenly his body went limp. Gwallter raised Dorcas's head tenderly.

'She's still alive. Look, I've a cart nearby. Help me carry her and I'll take her home.'

As if he had surrendered his will to the other, Shadrach obeyed. Before long Dorcas's inert body lay on the cart, and Gwallter did his best to cover her nakedness with warm straw.

'Where does she live? Do you know?'

Shadrach shook his head and mumbled something about Bryn Mawr. As if she had heard the name, Dorcas began to stir.

'Ellis . . . Ellis.'

'There you are, my girl,' said Gwallter. 'You're all right now.'

But she was tossing and turning where she lay. Gwallter jerked the pony's reins and started along Ffos y Felin towards Domen Fawr. When he turned round to look at Shadrach, he could see him standing stock still, staring after them, tears running down his cheeks.

She was lying on a white cloud lifted gently to and fro like a feather in the wind. At times the cloud was too hot and she had to fight to raise herself out of its heat. And then she was lying on mountains of ice, the pinnacles pushing painfully into her back. But she would not scream . . . she would not scream.

Another cloud hovered over her head and through it mysterious faces appeared and disappeared. Now and again she vaguely recognised a face. Who was that with the laughing eyes and wrinkles at each corner? Oh, she was so tired! Before she could remember, the face would vanish and another would take its place. A young face, hardly more than a child's, calling her name. And now, another, a man's, with thick freckles under his eyes. The rims of these eyes were red and she longed to tell him there was no need to cry. Let that pale, loving face stay near her always. She wanted to rise and wipe away those tears. She wanted to see the beloved smile return.

'Ellis . . . Ellis . . . Ellis.'

And now the black horse had returned, rearing its head towards the heavens, its breath rising like mist from its nostrils. But it was her own breath. She was safe while the horse continued to gaze upwards. One day it would lower its head down to her face and make its demand. She must keep some breath to fight on that day. And this was what she lacked. For her breath had been drowned in the Red Chair. Now her forehead was being seared by a cool hand whose touch purified her whole body. She opened her eyes to smile at him, a calm, peaceful smile.

'Ellis . . . '

Her eyes closed once more but this time the smile stayed on her lips.

6

Dorcas was buried at night in the new cemetery on Tyddyn-y-Garreg land. The plot had been given to the Friends by Lewis Owen and by now more than one lay there under the dark soil. Rowland noticed that Ellis went there very seldom, unless he went there unobserved. Outwardly he showed little distress but he rarely spoke and his features had become finer-drawn than ever. One night Rowland went over to the servants' loft to find someone to help him with a sick cow, but at the threshold, hand on the door-latch, he hesitated. From the far corner of the room came the sound of a muffled moaning.

The only time Ellis spoke was at Friends' Meetings and when his words broke on to the silence they urged love and compassion for the enemies of the Quakers. How much, wondered Rowland, did it cost him to speak in these terms? Did he have to force the words of forebearance from his lips in the hope that his true feelings would follow?

'I believe, O Lord. Help thou mine unbelief . . . '

Marged and Rowland were to be married in the autumn. But Dorcas and Ellis were also to have been married in the autumn and, out of regard for Ellis's feelings, they had suggested postponing their wedding. But Ellis would not hear of it.

'Dorcas will be sad if you do.'

When he did mention her at all, he spoke of her in the present, as though she were still with him, and there was a challenge in his eyes which silenced anyone who tried to contradict him.

Bereavement wraps its own shroud around those who are left behind, thought Rowland. Ellis was a stranger, his thoughts tightly enclosed within himself, and yet there was about him a certain new, profound tranquillity. For the first time, the master felt the servant to be the older of the two.

The harvest was poor that year. After an early spring it had been a rainswept summer, and Rowland surveyed the corn lying in the fields limp and sadly blackened, and the barns far from full of hay.

'Good weather for turnips and swedes,' comforted the old servant Dafydd, a countryman to the core, always prepared to accept what came. But the master of Bryn Mawr was only too aware of the importance of a good harvest that year, with so much cattle having been seized, and he looked unhappily at the wet devastation before him.

He mentioned his fears to Robert Owen, Dolserau, as they journeyed together to the Yearly Meeting in Montgomeryshire.

'I fear that it's not yet over. They will probably take every acre of the farm bit by bit, as well as the stock. There's no knowing where it will end.'

The other man did not reply. Rowland looked at him, his face slowly reddening.

'Things are the same with thee, too, my Friend, I know,' he murmured, a little shame in his voice.

'And for hundreds of others,' added Robert Owen. 'It's a terrifying prospect, my young friend, I know.'

'Don't misunderstand me, Robert Owen. I'm not likely to deny my belief. Only . . . only the most difficult thing is . . . to accept what comes quietly without retaliating or trying to defend oneself.'

'What else can one do but accept? And suffer?'

'But thou wert a soldier. How canst thou accept so much when thou hast been so accustomed to action?' He did not wait for a reply. 'There's something so wrong here. Hast thou heard that the persecution has died down in England? At the very time Dolgellau gaol is full to overflowing—'tis more full of Quakers than those slopes are full of sheep.'

They rode down Bwlch Oerddrws towards Dinas Mawddwy hoping to reach Dolobran before dawn. The quietly grazing sheep formed a yellow-white patchwork on the hills. Higher up, the peaks of the mountains were hidden in mist. Fine rain was falling again and Robert Owen shifted painfully in his saddle, drawing his cloak around him more tightly.

'Rheumatic?'

'Aye,' was the only reply but Rowland could see he was wincing with pain. The years in a damp prison had left their scars on the ex-soldier. Anger rose within him.

'What causes such hatred and cruelty in Dolgellau? 'Tis nothing new. I remember hearing my father tell of the days of Bloody Mary when they severed the breasts of women and girls in the town and men were tortured and burnt. And 'tis little better today.'

Halting his horse, he stared down unseeingly at the stream chattering noisily over the stones.

'If I could be sure their actions were prompted by conscience or by some devout allegiance to the Mother Church, it would be different. But it's not so. Lefi Huws, yes. He worships law and order. But the others . . . Dost thou sometimes feel that evil itself stalks over this magnificent land?'

'No. Not evil alone. Fear. And little imagination, perhaps, and this breeds intolerance. Sin is often the result of a want of imagination.'

'And jealousy and malice towards anyone who dares step out of line.'

'There are such places throughout the country. Dolgellau just happens to be one of them.'

After a brief silence he added: 'Perhaps it is the mountains around us that enclose the heart as well as the body.'

A shadow of a smile crossed Rowland's face.

'It's true that nearly all the Friends live high on the slopes of the mountains.'

There were thirty of them gathered at Dolobran. Rowland observed that their hosts, the two brothers Thomas and Charles Lloyd, spoke in English. He could not but admire their gentlemanly bearing, the fine chiselled features and lively, confident eyes. English was also the language of the Quakers from Nantmel in Radnorshire, and Tenby. But most of them spoke freely and naturally in Welsh and it was obvious that they were understood by all.

It was the sufferings of Friends that received the greatest attention. Each delegate in turn read out a long list of names and specific persecution suffered by each one. The lists were lengthy and sad. Yet, said Richard Davies of Newtown, the situation was not as hopeless as it had appeared to be at the last half-yearly meeting. Perhaps the end was in sight. Far from it, asserted Thomas Lloyd, and asked Robert Owen to report on the harsh treatment of the Quakers in Merioneth.

The tragedy of Dorcas was only one of many throughout the county. But as he listened to the recital, Rowland Ellis was forced to close his eyes, and when he tried to open them it seemed as though each eyelid had been caught in a spider's web. Once again his thoughts went over the ever-recurring question—Where would it all end? For Ellis, the Dolserau family, Marged, the children, for himself?

Thomas Lloyd's voice broke through his musing. He was speaking of George Fox.

'Praise God, the ill health that has beset him throughout the year is clearing and his strength is returning. He is now preparing to travel to Europe in the New Year, taking in Germany and the Low Countries. Several of the Friends will be going with him and we pray God for his protection and strength.'

He paused before continuing in a low, urgent voice.

'For some time, there have been among us those who have dreamed of a Holy Experiment in a far-off country. Consider, my Friends, a land where love reigns, where justice is sweetened with mercy, where men are free to worship as they please, where the Law is based on the divine light within, a kingdom of the earth become a kingdom of God and of His Christ. Across the Atlantic there are many territories as wild now as the Garden of Eden was before God breathed His holy spirit over it. If the Almighty leads us to these lands to establish a kingdom for the Children of Light, I think we shall not lack followers.'

The idea was not new to any of them. The dream was mentioned every time there was a Meeting in London. But this was the first time it had been talked about in Wales. After a thoughtful silence a woman spoke.

'Is not all this talk of a country over the sea but a wish to escape persecution? Should we not rather stay here to bear witness in the Lamb's War, accepting whatever may befall.'

But Thomas Lloyd had already considered this argument.

'You have all heard that oppression seems to be on the wane. None of us would have been prepared to run away when the battle was at its height. Is there need for stronger proof of our motives? The Pilgrim Fathers left these shores fifty years ago. The Baptists departed from Wales fifteen years ago. They were not accused of cowardice. We should be going not in order to escape but in order to prepare a new kingdom in readiness for the Day of the Lord.'

The golden sun of early autumn shone through the tall windows and lit up the face of the speaker. On the wall behind him shelves of books extended from ceiling to floor and over the carved fireplace another shelf ran from wall to wall sparkling with copper and gold ornaments.

It was difficult to remember in these cultured surroundings that the owner had spent ten years in Welshpool jail. And now, thought Rowland in wonder, he was contemplating leaving it all to start a new life some four thousand miles away.

The others also had mixed feelings. Robert Owen (of all people) sided with Thomas Lloyd, but Rowland could hardly blame him after all he had suffered. The Pembrokeshire and Nantmel Friends agreed with him as well. The ones from Caernarfon, Beaumaris and Denbigh were doubtful. The words of one Friend echoed Rowland's own thoughts. This man spoke excitedly, his arms flailing like a scythe.

'Some of you here are at home in the English language — more so perhaps than you are in Welsh. But you have only to listen to me for a short while to perceive that my English is poor — so, for that matter is the English of other Friends from Anglesey and Caernarfonshire. Can anyone tell me how we are going to cope with a new language as well as a new country?'

Thomas Lloyd smiled at him.

'The Friend is right to ask this question. This I can tell thee. The Welsh are to be allowed to remain together in one province, in a new Wales, cleaner and purer than the one we are in at present. And no man need change his customs nor those of his children.'

'But how can we be sure of that?' persisted the man from Caernarfon.

'Only by believing the word of Friends in London,' answered Thomas. 'And what better assurance could you wish for, my Friend?'

Rowland felt they were discussing something completely hypo-thetical—something that would never take place in their time. Thomas Lloyd could name neither time nor place, nor give any of the details that would remove the discussion from the realms of speculation into reality. He felt that the Friend from Caernarfon had raised premature bogeys. When it was over, the Meeting had done nothing to change any previously held conviction.

On his return home, all that had taken place at the Meeting was banished from his mind because of the amount of hard work which had to be done on the farm. But, as the autumn evenings grew longer and the leaves fell, the pace gradually slackened, and at last he had time to play with the children and notice how they were growing.

Marged was now the centre of their world. They spent as much time at Dyffrydan as at Bryn Mawr, more if anything. Rowland saw a gentle blush like apple blossom returning to Ann's cheeks. More wonderful still he saw rays of understanding begin to beam in Siân's eyes.

Marged would take them with her along the edge of the lake where the birch and willow bent towards the water. She taught them to know the cry of the curlew over the moors and they stood still with her watching the hawk hover before descending on its prey. They ran to her, clutching in their hands wild flowers that grew on the moorland, reciting their names after her . . . marsh-marigold, clover, cowslip, harebell, red campion . . .

Back at Dyffrydan the children had discovered a frog skulking near the doorstep. Ann jumped aside in fright but Siân had squat-ted down and was purring over the creature. Marged watched the child hold the frog carefully in her hand and totter on spindly legs towards the middle of the farm yard, where she let it go free. If love and patience could clear the mist from the little one's mind, then she had plenty of both to give, for Siân's sake certainly, but espe-cially for the sake of her father.

Marged Humphrey did not delude herself about Rowland's feelings towards her. She knew that he felt relaxed and at peace in her company and that he asked nothing more of her. If she longed for him to caress her cheek occasionally or touch her arm, or to see a flicker of passion suddenly light up in his eyes, she gave no sign. She was prepared to play the role he wanted of her—mother to his children, confidante, unruffled organiser, spiritual mate. She smothered the small voice that demanded to know how long this would be enough.

'Come, children. We must go home to Bryn Mawr.'

Siân came at once and clutched at her skirts. But Ann set up a commotion.

'Want to go to the cow shed to see uncle milking.'

'It's not milking time yet. Come.'

Ann was for going back to the lake to play. She had forgotten the name of one of the flowers and wanted to find it to show Marged. Every possible excuse was thought of to delay going home. Marged sighed. Of the two she found poor, simple Siân the easier to control.

'Very well. We must go without thee. It will be dark before long but no doubt thou wilt find the way.'

She took Siân's hand and forced herself not to look back nor to listen to the shout that followed her. The increasing nearness of the howls behind her proved that this time she had won.

The children ran to meet their father. They had now lost all shyness with him, apart from those times when he had been absent from home on long journeys. Then it took an hour or two for the stranger to be accepted again into their small circle and become their familiar father once more.

Marged stood in the shadow of the doorway watching the father with a daughter on each knee. I am outside this, she thought suddenly, her throat constricting. The three of them have forgotten about me.

She stepped inside the room and immediately Rowland put the children aside and rose to greet her.

'Come, Marged, thou art tired. Come and sit down.' He took her hands and drew her to the settle. The children had found a basket full of apples in the corner and had started playing with them.

'No, do not trouble. Let them play,' said Rowland as Marged sought to restrain them. 'I want to speak with thee.'

His hair has fallen over his forehead just as it had on the day I saw him carry Siân Morris's naked body. That was when I knew I loved him. His face is thinner now and the furrows between his brows are deeper, but he is the same. Siân Morris and the two of us beginning to want him at the same time. How she had pressed her body against his—and frightened him. And how I now long to feel his body against mine but am too afraid of frightening him.

His words and his manner were tender. The wind wailed against the window, a portent of rain. Flames leapt hungrily against the bars and the warmth from them mingled with a new-found happiness which set her heart aglow.

'I have been speaking with Ellis Puw tonight.'

Moments passed before he continued. She thought of Ellis, too. Something had died in him. But something else had been born.

'It was difficult to know how to talk of our wedding. But it was as if he knew what was in my mind. He said—'

Rowland closed his eyes. 'He said,"Dorcas and I are united in a way I never thought possible. There is no need for thee and Marged to worry about my feelings. I hope you will both marry soon."'

Marged felt the tears well in her eyes. Gently Rowland placed his hand under her chin and bent his head to kiss her. She stifled an overwhelming desire to throw her arms around him and hold him close to her.

But after all, their marriage did not take place that month. After the death of Dorcas, the Quakers had been left in peace, as if her drowning had somehow been a catharsis for the mob. But it was a truce that lasted too long to please the rector.

Up to now he had been able to depend upon the town's hooligans to create trouble for the Quakers. And if their enthusiasm put them on the wrong side of the law then that was not Morris Jones's business. But a great silence had descended as if everyone had decided to tolerate, if not accept, these peculiar creatures in their midst.

What worried the parson was his own delicate position. He

badly needed to do something to establish himself once again in the eyes of his patron. The last time it had come to Hywel Vaughan's ears that his parishioners had been obliged to carry their rector out of Church in the middle of morning service, he had felt the sharp edge of his tongue. Next time, warned Hywel Vaughan . . .

How to find a way of pleasing the Squire of Hengwrt? There was no need to ponder long, for the answer was clear. Morris Jones hated the Quakers because they had humiliated him personally and shown no respect for his office. But he knew that Hywel Vaughan's hatred went a hundred times deeper. What better way to re-instate himself and ensure his own personal safety than to be seen and heard attacking the enemies of his master?

The following Sunday in Church, he read out the names of those who had not attended service during that month. Or at least of some who had not. He omitted the names of the Independents, the Baptists, the Antinomians and the Socinians. Others conveniently listed together were named—Quakers every one.

7

Their prison was a cellar underneath the Court House. A cold damp rose from the stone steps leading down to it, but in the cell itself this was the least unpleasant of the smells. The only light came through a window near the ceiling—a window without glass but firmly barred. A passer-by outside could bend down and stare at the prisoners through the bars. Children found great amusement in doing this.

There were ten of them in this cell, seven men and three women—with two beds to be shared among everyone. For these beds the jailor charged seven shillings each, hinting that worse might be in store for those who could not or would not pay.

They started trying to bring some kind of order to their lives by placing the beds for the women in the far corner of the cell, the men making do with the small amount of straw at their disposal on the floor. When it rained and the wind whipped inside from the south-east, everyone had to take shelter at the farther end of the cell. The rain soon penetrated the earthen floor and there was barely enough straw to cover the sodden patches. Occasionally the jailor would bring a comparatively fresh bundle of straw but more often than not he was as deaf to their appeals as Cader Idris itself.

Rowland hated seeing Marged, Gainor Ifan, and Jane Owen struggle along day after day to keep themselves reasonably clean. The jailor refused to bring them water, unless they paid him an exorbitant sum of money.

There was one advantage in their exposed situation. Lisa and others could bring them clean garments, food and even books, thrusting them through the window. This was a dangerous service, for the jailor took great exception to being robbed of his only livelihood. One young girl who had been caught at this immediately found herself in jail with the others. But Lisa persisted. After the death of Dorcas she had spent hours in solitary weeping, not knowing exactly whether her tears were a longing for Dorcas, repentance for her sins, or fear of the flames of hell. But all at once she found it was she and she alone who had to look after the children at Bryn Mawr, with no one but old Dafydd and Tomos the servant from Bwlch-coch to see to the farm and the livestock. The realisation worked on her like a miracle. She cleaned the house from top to bottom, fed the children, mended their clothes and rushed backwards and forwards to town fetching and carrying for the prisoners as well as she was able.

However inconvenient it was for the women, it would have been much worse, Rowland told himself, if they had all been in solitary confinement. At least they were able to take strength from one another's company. The stench, the dark crippling cold and the endless frenzied screaming of the old whore in the next cell would have been hard to bear alone.

Rowland studied the faces around him. Jane Owen with dozens of newly-etched lines round her mouth and eyes, her skin like thin parchment, but her serenity a steady light brightening the gloom. Young Gainor Ifan, separated from her husband who was in another jail. Sometimes she would sit motionless as a statue, hands folded, refusing all food. At other times she would chatter on endlessly—about her children, about her cat Dafydd, about her Aunt Sioned—until the others longed to put their fingers in their ears and scream at her to stop.

Just now she was pleating her skirt, all her attention directed towards making each pleat exactly the same size as the other. As the pleats became too bulky to hold between her fingers, she would let them go and start all over again.

Marged stood under the window so that the dwindling daylight might fall on the book in her hand. A tiny smile played round her mouth as she read, lost to her surroundings. The wind played hide-and-seek through the bars, ruffling her plaited hair. The outline of her body was becoming blurred as the light diminished. Rowland saw how long and slender her neck was, how straight her back and how tender the swell of her bosom. Marged would be a perfect mother for his children he reflected for the hundredth time. But for the first time the notion that perhaps they would have children of their own entered his thoughts. A desire to touch her came over him, and he was about to cross over to her when he remembered that the imprisoned community had erected a barrier between the men and the women, as impregnable as it was imaginary.

One week became two and two merged into a month. As the year drew to its end, the cell became colder and colder. At first the sickening smell of sweat and excrement had been the hardest to bear. But this discomfort was gradually forgotten in the greater sufferings brought on by the severe cold.

Edward Prys, Dôl-gun, was wracked with a cough which got worse every day. One of the beds had been dragged over to the men's side for him, and there came a day when he was unable to get up from it. The warder refused to provide a blanket and before dawn broke the next day the old man was dead.

His body was removed in a sack and for the first time Gainor Ifan broke down and wept uncontrollably. Marged and Jane did their best to comfort her but the severe cold, the filth and the restriction were too much for her. All day and night she moaned until at last she fell into an uneasy stupor.

As the others listened helplessly, each prayed for self-control while every nerve in their bodies cried out to follow her example and let go. Ellis was the one who eventually quietened her. Crossing over to her part of the cell, he placed his hand on her hot forehead. She shivered with a tremor that ran right through her body and then, with a deep sigh, became perfectly still. Marged, sitting beside her, thought she was dead, but Ellis whispered that she was sleeping. He knelt in the straw at her side.

'Thou hast a remarkable gift, Ellis Puw,' said Rowland, remembering Steffan. 'Thou shouldst be a doctor.'

Ellis smiled. 'One must have learning to be a doctor.' He added, after a pause, 'I remember hearing that my mother had the gift to help the sick.'

'But thou couldst not possibly have learnt it from her. She died at thy birth.'

Rowland's thoughts turned to his daughter Siân. If children inherited their parents' characteristics without even having known them, what had Siân inherited from the mother she had never seen?

Slowly he had been forced to face the knowledge that his daughter was not quite normal. Was this the meaning of the sins of the fathers being visited on their children? Who was to blame? It was difficult to believe that God punished man through His children.

His soul cried out against such blasphemy. And he *must* love God. Siân's very condition made it imperative for him to hold on to a belief in the Creator's mercy. Any other way led to despair, to a world and life without meaning.

One day he had returned home, and, hearing screams filling the air, he had run upstairs convinced that thieves or assassins had broken in. But there was no one to be seen but Siân and Ann. Ann had been standing behind the door staring at her sister, tears of fright pouring down her cheeks. In her arms she was holding a rag doll dressed in a frilly cap and shawl. But the screaming had come from Siân, not Ann. She had stood there facing the wall, banging another rag doll against it in a frenzy, spattering it with sawdust from the doll's inside, all control lost.

'Siân!' But he had hardly been able to hear his own voice. Then he had felt someone rush past him and had seen Marged gather the child up and whisper in her ear. Siân had then turned her face towards Marged and started to cry more naturally. Slowly Marged had soothed her, and later Ann told him what had caused the outburst. Marged had given the girls a doll each as a present. They were both identically dressed in skirt, apron and shawl, and the little girls had enjoyed dressing and undressing them in turn. Siân could always undress her doll fairly easily but failed pitifully every time she attempted to put the clothes on again. Although she tried to imitate Ann's actions, she had no idea at all how to dress the doll. Each time she tried she became more and more furious and finally turned her fury on the doll itself.

Rowland sighed quietly. That time Marged had been there to comfort her. But what if the same thing happened again without Marged there? He prayed that Lisa would be patient, and wise enough to know what to do.

The next day soldiers came to escort them on foot to Bala to stand trial before Judge Walcott.

As soon as they saw the Judge frowning at them across the court room, they knew they could expect little mercy, and his first words confirmed their fears. In charging them he cited an old law from the reign of Mary Tudor—'that they were directly or indirectly guilty of introducing a foreign power into the country and creating imperium in imperio by adhering to a foreign practice instead of obeying the law of the Sovereign. And further that they urged the supremacy of the Pope over the English crown.'

Rowland was so weary after walking the eighteen miles to Bala and so concerned about the sufferings of the women, he found it difficult to concentrate on the Judge's words. There had been little sleep for them before appearing in Court. His heart sank as he heard again the familiar lies incorporated in the charge of praemunire. He knew only too well what the punishment would be. Their lands and possessions would be seized by the Crown.

He was surprised to discover that the prospect did not cause him as much pain as it would have in the past. Gradually he must have been preparing himself for this day from the time he had first joined the Quakers. In one way the knowledge that it was to happen gave him a sense of freedom. He was young and Marged would be at his side with her love and encouragement. Perhaps indeed they could make a fresh start elsewhere.

This was the first time he had even remotely considered going to America. Thomas Lloyd's words must have fallen on more fertile ground than he had imagined. But how could he leave this land?

The Clerk was now commanding them to take the Oath, and an interpreter rose to translate the request into Welsh. In the silence that followed the Friends looked straight at the Judge without uttering a word. He bellowed across the court room that the law of the land demanded they obey. Rowland's voice could be heard low but clear.

'If our creed permitted us to swear any oath, it would be one of allegiance to King Charles since we deny the supremacy of the Pope. But everyone present in this court room today knows well by now that we believe that inasmuch as Christ commanded us swear not, we must obey that command, even though we give our bodies to be burned . . . '

The Judge interrupted him.

'Are you suggesting that there are no Christians in any other sect but your own?'

'There are many good people who call themselves Christian.'

'You avoid the question. Do you believe that these good people are Christians?'

Silence fell on the Court. Everyone knew that the fate of the prisoners depended on his reply. They also knew it would be a test of the Quaker's integrity.

'No person who disobeys the Lord's commandments is a Child of the Light.'

All eyes were now turned with eager expectancy on the Judge, who addressed the jury.

'Men of the jury, you heard what the prisoner had to say. I leave you to judge for yourselves the measure of blasphemy contained in those words. If you consider the prisoner to be speaking the truth, then you will find him not guilty. If you consider him not to be speaking the truth, then he is a liar and not only must his evidence be dismissed but his motives in uttering such falsehoods must be examined. You are aware that there are powers at work in this land today threatening our Protestant traditions, conspiring secretly to undermine our constitutional system. Consider carefully and deliver your verdict before God. Are these prisoners guilty or not guilty?'

The reply was immediate. 'Guilty.'

The Judge nodded his head in approval. He waited for silence and then delivered his sentence.

'This Court sentences the men to be hanged, drawn and quartered and the women to be burnt at the stake.'

A long-drawn out sigh rustled through the room. Everyone was stunned. It was one thing to punish the foolish creatures but to put them to death was another matter entirely. They all stared at the Judge in disbelief but he had risen to his feet to order the prisoners to be taken away.

The Judge was the Judge and his was the last word. Gradually most of them were beginning to accept that this was the law of the land and that they could do nothing about it. By tomorrow the edge of their shock would have subsided. Few of them had ever before had a chance of seeing a hanging or a burning and already excitement was beginning to rise in some at the prospect of a new experience.

As for the Friends, they stood motionless, like creatures bound by strong cords. Months, even years of imprisonment they were prepared for, but this was unbelievable. Gainor Ifan slumped to the floor. Jane Owen's lips moved slowly but this was the only sign she gave of distress. Marged turned to Rowland and the message of love in her eyes melted the coldness in his heart. Then she knelt by Gainor to try to console her.

A commotion at the rear of the Court room was now diverting attention from the prisoners. Rowland turned to follow the gaze of the others. Then his interest became more acute. He could see the tall figure of Thomas Lloyd, Dolobran, thrusting his way through the crowd. Following him was a middle-aged man, a stranger, dressed in the garb of King's Counsel. Thomas Lloyd shouted as he pressed forward.

'My Lord Judge, I beg leave to speak in this case. Or rather —' indicating his companion, 'I beg leave for Counsellor Corbett to deliver his message.'

Then at that moment it was as if the Court room held only Judge Walcott and Counsellor Corbett, two long-standing enemies in the law. Walcott remembered with bitterness how the previous year he had been defeated in Worcester in the case of George Fox, and now some ill-star had brought this Counsellor to Bala, no doubt for the same purpose.

'The verdict has been given. There is nothing more to be said.'

'Your pardon, m'lord, but there is more to be said. I am here at the behest of Judge Hale—the Chief Justice,' he added with significant emphasis.

Walcott sat down heavily.

'You should have come before this, Mr. Corbett,' he mumbled gruffly.

Corbett replied, 'For some reason, m'lord—and perhaps it is you who would know why—it was impossible to acquire a copy of the indictment against these prisoners. The message from the Chief Justice concerns the indictment and the sentence.'

Walcott began to lose his temper and his voice rose.

'How can your message be concerned with either the indictment or the sentence when you were not in attendance at the hearing?'

'Because I have reason to believe, m'Lord, that you are labouring under a legal misapprehension. As you were before.'

A murmur of astonishment went through the Court at the temerity of this Counsellor. Silence fell as the gathering waited intently to hear the Judge's reactions.

'M'Lord,' said Corbett, not waiting for the reply, his voice resounding throughout the Court room. 'You have no power to execute man or woman on a charge of *praemunire*—the charge of conspiring to introduce a foreign power into the country.'

'And may I ask why not, Counsellor?'

'Because in so doing you are acting on the Law of *Praemunire* of 1392, that is, the Law *De Heretico Comburendo*. And the penalty of death for that crime was abolished by the Act of Supremacy 1562.'

A cold gleam came into the Judge's eyes. He leaned forward from the bench.

'True. True. But refusal to take the oath of supremacy is treasonable. And you, Mr. Corbett, know the punishment for treason.'

'Yes?' queried Corbett, smiling.

The Judge lost his patience completely and repeated at the top of his voice.

'Yes, Mr. Counsellor. I will tell you. The prisoner to be borne on a hurdle to the place of execution and hanged by the neck until almost dead, then to be cut down and while still alive his entrails to be plucked out and burnt before his eyes. His head will be severed and his body cut into four quarters. And in accordance with His Majesty's pleasure . . . '

'No!' The single word broke across the other's tirade like a sword. 'No, m'Lord. Not in accordance with His Majesty's pleasure.'

Corbett unfolded a scroll of parchment and handed it to the Judge.

'You will see that His Gracious Majesty and his Parliament have seen fit to rescind that law. And the message I convey from the Chief Justice is that he is astonished, m'Lord, at your persistence in administering it. He feels that the only explanation must be that your personal animosity towards this sect which call themselves Quakers has rendered you both blind and deaf.'

It seemed as if everyone had forgotten how to breathe, so still was the Court Room. A fisherman in the street outside shouted his wares and the normal sound intruded strangely on the unreality of the interior. Slowly the Judge drew his hand across his eyes, then gazed long and silently at Corbett before admitting defeat. When at last the words came they were forced out as reluctantly as a limpet dragged from a rock.

'In the light of this information, the indictment against the defendants is withdrawn. Release the prisoners, constables!'

Rowland once again had the sensation that all this had happened before, that he was taking part in a drama with words and actions well-rehearsed. He knew before it happened that Gainor would start laughing and crying, and that Marged would chide her with unusual firmness. He knew that the crowd in the Court would yell and clap their hands and rush to congratulate Counsellor Corbett.

Thomas Lloyd was crossing towards them.

'Carriages are waiting outside. We will take you all straight to your homes.'

The man from Dolobran sounded jubilant.

'Thomas Lloyd —' began Rowland but the other interrupted him.

'Say nothing now, Friend. There will be time enough to talk later.' He placed his hand on Rowland's shoulder. 'I hope—no, I'm sure—that this will put an end to our tribulations for a time, at least.' He turned to speak with some of the others, urging them to hurry out to the waiting carriages. Rowland felt someone squeeze his hand. He turned and solemnly raised Marged's fingers to his lips.

8

Thomas Lloyd had predicted well. Without fully appreciating it at the time, Rowland and the Friends were to look back on the four or five years following their release as an interlude of peace. Shortly after the case at Bala, Judge Walcott died—of hate said some who knew of his persecution of the Quakers. But his severity had one unexpected sequel. A wave of sympathy for the once scorned sect spread through Penllyn, Edeyrnion and Dolgellau. Toleration was now the keynote. Though people still jeered at the sober dress, the hat stuck on the head as if nailed down, the refusal to bow, the 'theeing and thouing', something akin to admiration had crept into the laughter.

If these people were prepared to face imprisonment and possibly death for their peculiar beliefs, there must be some strange power in their creed. Men, women and children began to flock to their meetings, most of them out of curiosity, but some from a real desire to know more. And more and more stayed with them.

In February 1678 Rowland and Marged were married and early the following year their first child was born. Rowland wanted to call him Ellis after his own father, Ellis ap Rhys, but eventually he agreed with Marged that the boy should be named Rowland. He observed gratefully that the birth of her own child had made not the slightest difference to Marged's care for her two step-children. And they in turn, were devoted to their little brother—and their sister. For now they had Beth, too, just one week old.

Rowland stood at the bottom of the path, his elbow resting on the top bar of the gate. Gazing up at the house, he gave a deep sigh of contentment. Plentiful harvests, Meetings sweet as cooling streams, the forbearance of his neighbours and the memories of the winter of 1676 now only a hideous nightmare: he wanted everyone around him to share his happiness. And so they did. He smiled as he remembered coming upon Lisa in the arms of the young servant Tomos Owen. Tomos would be a good husband to her, a man of few words but as loyal and trustworthy as his predecessor had been cunning and unre!iable.

It was a pity that Ellis had not taken up with Lisa, but perhaps it would have been too painful for him with its inevitable memories. Rowland found himself worrying less and less about Ellis. In fact, worrying would have been a presumption in the face of his gentle composure. Those who remembered the diffident, uncertain boy, were struck now by the quiet assurance he had developed. After his release from prison, he had travelled around preaching fearlessly. Had it not been for the new spirit of toleration everywhere, he would certainly have found himself back in jail. His was a simple message. Rowland knew the words almost as well as did Ellis himself. One thing only was needed: to recognise the voice of Christ within, who was the true shepherd, and to follow Him in all things towards everlasting life.

Rowland could hear that surprisingly rich voice now, rising like a torrent from the rather frail body.

'Yet some poor ignorant folk say,"We know nothing. We can only believe the learned men and what they teach us. For they read and have knowledge." But that way thou wilt never become one of Christ's flock, for if the fishermen and the unlettered men of old had listened only to the men of learning, they would never have believed in Christ and become His followers . . . '

The rain sweeping across his shoulders, his red hair dripping under the round hat, the shadows of its wide brim underlining the paleness of his face—but the sincerity of Ellis's words as he spoke transcended everything else. His voice echoed from the outer walls of the Church, where at every opportunity he preached to the people as they made their way to St. Mary's.

Where I have sinned unheedingly
I pray thy grace will me restore
And swear that I intend to tread
Those paths of wickedness no more

Without thy help I can do nought
But as the swine roll in the mud,
God cleanse me of my evil ways
And turn my soul to good.

Two men were riding towards Rowland from the direction of Coed y Pandy but in the gathering darkness he could not make them out until they were within a hundred yards of him. Then he rushed forward to welcome them.

'John ap John, Thomas Lloyd, I'm overjoyed to see you. Come into the house. Marged will be delighted if you sup with us.'

He sensed their message must be urgent to bring them all the way to see him like this. There was about them an excitement which they were, for the time being, striving hard to control. But he ignored this until they were seated at the table. Having attended to their food, Marged made for the door, saying she was sure the three had private matters to discuss. But John ap John insisted that she stayed.

'Our message concerns thee as well, Marged.'

She returned and sat with them at the table, the light from the lamp reflecting the visitors' eager faces.

'This is what I have to say,' John began. 'You know we have from time to time discussed the prospect of a Holy Experiment in a place where we can establish a community founded on the truth which has been revealed to us.'

Rowland could feel his heart beat faster and instinctive rebellion rise within him.

'I was in London about a month ago and there I talked with William Penn,' continued John looking straight into Rowland's eyes, challenging him.

'Somehow, Friend, I see the Lord's hand leading us towards this new kingdom He has ordained for us.'

John had therefore changed his mind. Or perhaps it would be fairer to say that he had now made up his mind. For Rowland suddenly remembered he had not offered any opinion one way or the other when the suggestion had first been made in his hearing. He knew of Thomas Lloyd's enthusiasm from the outset and was not surprised to find him listening intently, with a smile of encouragement.

William Penn (said John) had acquired a large tract of land in New England, between Massachusetts and Virginia— something to do with a debt from the King to his father, Admiral Penn. He saw this as an opportunity to establish the sort of community the Friends had been longing for. From his pocket he drew out a piece of paper and smoothed it carefully on the table.

'He is prepared—nay, he desires—to divide his land into tracts for sale to Friends at reasonable prices.'

John began to read from the paper in his careful English with a strong Welsh accent.

'To such persons as are inclined to the province, such is the expense a man with £100 cash would be under if he bought 500 acres and transported himself, wife, a child and two menservants. It being understood that 500 acres of uncleared land is equivalent to 50 acres of cleared English or Welsh land.

'By taking along certain small articles, cloth, clothes, harness, implements, etc., and selling them there, the land will be paid for by the fifty percent profit derived. The transportation of the party would cost not more than £38. 2. 6d. with new clothes, skirts, hats, shoes, stockings and drawers, a ton of things to sell and four gallons of brandy and twenty-four pounds of sugar for the voyage.'

Rowland felt inclined to interrupt and ask, 'What has this to do with us? I have already indicated that I have not the slightest interest in the project.' But in spite of himself he did feel a flicker of interest stirring as he listened to John's precise voice. He glanced at Marged but her face betrayed none of her true feelings.

'Arriving at the purchase in early summer, encamping and clearing fifty acres for ploughing, cutting out best timber for house, according to directions, planting, erecting the log cabin and getting in the crops brings the experience of this party up to winter when the prospect is not so pleasant as they have only green wood to burn.'

The voice went on and Rowland marvelled at the detailed nature of the letter—from instructions on how to build a cabin thirty feet long and eighteen feet wide to the possible yield that could be expected from the land.

With all the seizure of land and stock he had suffered over the years, Rowland had seen his farm decrease to the size of a smallholding and the farmer in him responded to what he was hearing.

'But these estimates are misleading,' he objected. 'One must have a barn as well as a house.'

Thomas Lloyd broke in. 'According to this calculation, the cost of a house and barn together would be £15.10.0 and £24.10.0 for stock. William Penn has consulted thoroughly with farmers and lawyers before committing his information to paper and I must admit that the prospects give me great joy.'

But John could see he was proceeding too fast.

'No need for you to make an immediate decision. Our purpose in coming here was merely to present the plan to a number of good Friends and ask them to consider the offer very carefully. Will you both promise to do this?'

Rowland rose from his seat and crossed over to the window. He stood there with his back to the others, looking out into the darkness. The other two men exchanged glances and remained quiet until he turned towards them again.

'But why must we go so far away? Why cannot we carry out the Holy Experiment in our own country? There's a new spirit spreading through the land, and the people are eager to hear us. Why should we leave our homes and our neighbours and uproot ourselves, now of all times?'

He is softening towards them, thought Marged. He is seeking convincing answers to his own doubts. She saw his eyes searching the faces of the two men, looking for the message he hoped to find there, and something cold clutched at her.

'Things are not as peaceful as we all have believed, Rowland Ellis,' said Thomas Lloyd. 'Hast thou heard of a man called Titus Oates? How he claimed last year to have discovered a Papist plot to assassinate the King? God knows what his intention was for everyone knew he was lying. But as always when a rumour of this

171

sort is spread about someone uses it for his own purpose and takes it as an excuse to begin the persecution all over again. They have already arrested Lord Stafford for being, so they say, involved in the plot and he will almost certainly be executed. I need not tell thee how such a happening in far away London may be used as a weapon against those who do not conform to the Church of England. And the effects of this will be felt in Merioneth before long.'

'But thou hast said thyself, Thomas Lloyd, that it would be wrong for us to flee from persecution.'

Thomas frowned with a hint of impatience, if it could be said that a man of his serenity possessed such a weakness, but John ap John broke in: 'True. But there's another consideration and this is what troubles William Penn. He has been given this land and must make use of it. It is rich and fertile and there is a danger it will attract settlers with worldly interests if it be offered on the open market.'

Thomas said: 'William Penn sees a chance of using this gift for the glory of God and His Kingdom by confining it to the Children of Light. If we do not accept the challenge, this plan, which must have been inspired by God Himself, will fail, and all this fertile land will fall into the hands of men of this world.'

'So it is our duty to leave our homes to satisfy the whims of William Penn!'

The three men turned towards Marged, surprised at the unaccustomed sharpness in her voice.

'No, Marged Ellis. William Penn has a holy vision,' said Thomas. 'There is no call for us to judge him. He does not force anyone to go. He is offering us this opportunity, and we have the right to refuse if we so wish.'

'Of course we have,' replied Marged. 'And I will tell thee what is going to happen now. Some of us will accept the challenge— perhaps because we are seduced by the vision. Others of us will go because we are afraid of the future. And there will be some of us— oh, let us face this honestly—who will go because we, even the Children of Light, are influenced by tales of fertile lands. And a remainder will be left behind, as has happened from the days of the prophet Isaiah onwards, but a remainder weakened and impotent. And when these few remaining leaves have withered no more will grow in this part of the world— ever again. We will have forfeited our inheritance. Without reason. Don't you see? We have no choice now, have we? If we are to remain together, strong and persuasive, we must all go.'

Rowland had never heard Marged speak so. He stretched his hand across the table to touch hers, and the four of them fell into silence as if at a Meeting. Marged alone looked drained of all strength. It was John who eventually broke the silence.

'Love of country is a strange thing. I would not hurt thy feelings, Marged Ellis, but it is a love that can sometimes cloud one's judgment. All I would say to you both now is, wait on the Lord and follow wherever He leads. If then you still believe it is His wish that you must refuse this offer—then so be it.'

He rose to his feet and Thomas Lloyd followed. Marged did her utmost to shake herself free from a strange lethargy that had overtaken her, but they refused her invitation to stay the night, for they wished to speak with the Dolserau family. In bidding them farewell, Rowland felt that he and Marged had disappointed them sorely.

9

The great rush to buy had begun. The Gwanas brothers had each bought 182 acres. Ellis Morris, Dôl-gun Ucha, had ventured on 78 acres and Ifan ap William from Llanfachreth some 156 acres.

The small band of Quakers was beginning to disintegrate, as Marged had predicted, breaking up without having moved a yard from their homes. As soon as Meeting was over, the talk would immediately be of latest developments. Few facts were available and there was much speculation as to where exactly the location of the land would be and how it would be apportioned.

Rowland Ellis listened with mixed feelings as they talked hopefully of their dreams.

'What worries me,' he said to his wife, 'is how in the world a man like Ifan ap William can hope to sell his produce when he hasn't even a smattering of English. There's no certainty there will be another Welshman within a hundred miles of him.'

Others were also worried about this. Jane Owen, Dolserau, knew that Robert had set his heart on joining the Experiment in spite of his age. Their third son, Gruffydd, was as eager to go as his father was and, since he was a doctor, there was special pressure on him to join the company for everyone realised that the worst part of the venture would be the long voyage across, and a doctor was likely to be the most important person to serve their needs. But Rowland's fears troubled the Dolserau family as well.

'If only we could get William Penn to promise that the Welsh should all remain together,' said Gruffydd. 'Does anyone know whether he has said any more about this?'

'To a man of his class the Welsh language is barbaric,' said Rowland, his thoughts returning to his schooldays. 'It's hardly likely he will make special arrangements for us, especially since the aim of the Experiment is community living.'

'He was born in Ireland,' said Jane Owen. 'Their language is different, so perhaps he has more sympathy with us than we imagine.'

'Why not ask him then?'

Rowland continued to discuss the matter without committing himself or his family. But he was beginning to be affected by their enthusiasm. For him, of course, the idea was impossible. Who would look after Bryn Mawr, and how could Marged travel with four children and another expected? In any event, he knew Marged's sentiments, so that was an end to it. But the talk continued endlessly—about the gentle climate, the fertile soil, the streams and meadows, the fruitful harvests from the rich plains, the walnut and horse-chestnut trees, the plums and mulberries, sloes, grapes, hemp and hops all this talk he brought home to Marged, in spite of himself, and for the first time in his life he looked on the bareness of the hilly slopes of Cader Idris, weighed them in the balance and found them wanting.

'Penn seems to be a fair man,' continued Rowland. 'He will surely give you a hearing. Tell him you intend to remain a Welsh colony within his territory.'

The suggestion was worth following, everyone agreed. At least it would help allay the fears of the less educated among them. When the idea was passed on to John he was enthusiastic.

'If you compose a letter I will willingly deliver it to William Penn. But since I do not myself intend to go to America it would be better if one of you were with me.'

Finally it was decided that the doctor should accompany John and the letter was written.

' . . . For we declare with an open face to God and man that we desire to be by ourselves for no other End or purpose but that we might live together as a Civil Society, to endeavour to decide all controversies and debates among ourselves in a Gospell order, and not to entangle ourselves with Laws in an unknown tongue, as also to preserve our Language that we might ever keep Correspondence with our friends in the land of our Nativity. '

To the surprise of some and the joy of all, Penn agreed with alacrity. He said he had sought the Governor's permission to name the territory 'New Wales' but that the Secretary of the Council, a Welshman, had opposed this.

When Marged heard that the name agreed upon was to be Pennsylvania, she observed, 'Tis little surprise to me to hear that man give his own name to the land.'

'Marged, thou art always suspicious of William Penn—and yet thou hast never seen him.' But there was a smile in Rowland's eyes.

'Dost 'ee remember thy first letter to me from London? The description of him was so vivid, like a lamp illuminating every corner of his character.'

'I can't remember exactly what I said.'

'Everything I have heard about him since confirms that picture: proud, brave, but unimaginative and cunning.'

'Marged!'

'Oh, I know well enough that he has agreed to what the Welsh ask. But there's nothing in writing. Remember, that come what may, he wants to people his land—and if with Friends so much the better.'

'Thou art doing him less than justice. I happen to know it was the King that pressed him to accept the name Pennsylvania. Penn himself was not at all happy about it.'

But Marged was not convinced. 'Everyone will be sorry, mark my words.'

Her husband watched as she suckled the baby Beth, while Rowland crawled at her feet. He realised that a mixture of emotions led her to speak in this way, mostly because of her fear of a possible threat to the harmony and stability of her family. He knew that Marged felt that things were good as they were: the farm slowly returning to prosperity, the servants dependent on them for their daily sustenance, the children most time content, the persecution over.

Kneeling at her side, he caught hold of his son to prevent him crawling too far away. He wanted to reassure her that he, at least, would never leave Bryn Mawr, but the words stuck in his throat. He could no longer bind himself by any such assurance. Every time a traveller returned to London from Pennsylvania, he found himself hanging on his words, drinking deep of tales of massive forests, acres of plantations, streams and glow worms with light enough to guide the wanderer at night.

At last it was Lisa who gave him the final, fateful jolt.

By now she was nineteen years old, the lines of experience and suffering already etched on her face but her body still as soft and round as before. The servant Tomos had brought the spirit back into the lift of her head, and she smiled more readily in his company than she had done for years. One day she came to Rowland with the news that she and Tomos were to be married.

'Good,' said he. 'When?'

'Well, that depends on . . . we wanted to ask something first.'

'Yes?'

'There's a rumour that you are all going to Pennsylvania with the others,' said Lisa, her words tumbling out eagerly. 'Is it true?'

Rowland hesitated, not knowing what to say. He had had no idea how his servants would react to the notion. The surprising fact was that after all the talk and discussion he himself did not know the answer.

'Truly, Lisa, I do not know. It would mean selling Bryn Mawr— selling or leaving a bailiff to look after it.'

But this was not good enough. He would have to decide. She was waiting for an honest reply to her question. He made a great effort to choose his words as carefully as if he were before a judge.

'The Friends must remain together, this is imperative, and a spiritual community is more important than country, traditions, birth: all these are of the world. The truth we must face is that three quarters of our members intend to buy land in Pennsylvania and have had a promise from William Penn that they may remain as one entity. What is our duty, Lisa?'

But it was his own conscience he addressed and not the girl.

'Is it to support the Holy Experiment wherever God dictates?'

'Tomos and I were wondering whether we could come, too?'

Lisa's voice broke in as gently as a moth striking against his face.

177

'But Lisa art thou sure that thou—that you both wish to go so far? What about thy mother?'

'We couldn't go far enough away from this place.' Her low words sounded bitter. 'And as for Mother she'll be all right now.' There was something unsaid in her tone.

'What dost thou mean?'

But a veil had dropped over Lisa's face and she refused to say more than, 'Tis not for me to tell.'

Rowland's mind was preoccupied with a new idea that had suddenly struck him. If he were to buy some land now he would not need to go there himself, not at once—not at all, unless circumstances forced him to. What if Tomos and Lisa should go over with the first settlers to prepare the way before he finally gave up Bryn Mawr? Then if the Experiment failed, they could all return to Bryn Mawr. Nothing would have been lost. If, however, the Experiment succeeded, Marged, he and the children could go over when the youngest children were old enough to travel.

'What wouldst thou say if I bought land there and sent thee and Tomos to see what it was like?'

As he explained the scheme to Lisa, he felt a twinge of conscience realising that he was discussing this with the maid before consulting his wife, but he had said enough for his words to show their effect on Lisa.

Her shining eyes were all he needed to see. Two people, at least, will be happy, he thought ruefully, as he went in search of Marged.

She was standing at the top of the stairs looking out through the window, the outline of her figure silhouetted by the moonlight. Rowland drew in a quick breath. For a moment he imagined it was Meg who stood there the same bearing, the same long hair falling over her shoulders, the same breasts full with milk. She would turn in the darkness, whisper 'Roli' and beg for the ribbon he had promised her from the fair, and he once again twenty-two, his blood surging with longing for the nearness of his wife's body.

But it was not Meg whispering at the top of the stairs. Marged's voice was clear.

'Do not be afraid to tell me.'

'Marged!'

178

He began to climb towards her but felt unsteady. She held out her hands.

'Lisa told me she was going to ask thee. I saw her speaking with thee before I came upstairs.'

Rowland held her close.

'What didst thou tell Lisa?'

Marged turned her face to him, her lips searching for his.

'What didst thou tell Lisa?' he repeated.

'I told her thou wouldst be pleased to have another reason for buying land in Pennsylvania like the others.'

For one uncomfortable moment he felt she was laughing at him but her warmth and closeness denied this.

Once he had made a decision he felt a great sense of freedom. All his problems fell into place one by one like a child's puzzle completed. The sooner he went to Dolserau to tell Dr. Gruffydd Owen of his intentions the better, so that his name could be added to the daily-lengthening list.

Ellis was sharpening his scythe when Rowland came to explain his plans to him. He began diffidently, for he had never heard Ellis talk of leaving and he did not know how he felt about it. The younger man listened in silence.

'Naturally thou wilt miss Tomos and Lisa,' ended Rowland, rather lamely. 'But we will be here for some time—that is, if we go at all.'

Ellis was still sharpening his scythe.

'Dost thou hear me, Ellis? What dost thou say?'

Ellis looked up. 'Yes, of course I do. I was just thinking.' The swift blush had crept into his cheeks.

'I was thinking . . . Could I bring a wife with me when we go to America?'

'A wife, Ellis Puw'?'

'Well, yes. She would be a great help in the house and on the land if need be.'

This was the last thing he had expected to hear and Rowland laughed aloud with pleasure.

'Well, thou sly fox, Ellis. Who is she? Do I know her?'

Ellis returned to his sharpening and said, 'Sinai Robarts.'

Rowland opened his mouth in astonishment but Ellis looked up at him suddenly, an appeal in his eyes. Silence fell between them, then Ellis spoke.

'She is very much alone, Rowland Ellis. And what will become of her? Dorcas and Steffan have gone. Lisa is about to marry. Gutyn and Sioned have found good positions but Dafydd, Huw, Lowri and Ellyw are left. What will become of them? I can look after them and I have a little money saved.'

There was nothing to say. Rowland's reactions were too confused as he looked down at Ellis sharpening the scythe as if his life depended on it. Rowland felt the pathos of it, but it had its funny side too, a young man marrying a woman with nine children, one of them his own Dorcas. Then it dawned on him that this was a reasonable and fitting solution for them both. Ellis was wedded to Dorcas as truly as if she were still alive, and Ellis and Sinai were inevitably bound together through her.

He put his hand on Ellis's shoulder and said slowly: 'You may come wherever I go. And Sinai too.'

The long journey was over and the little band of Quakers from Merioneth stood at the quayside with Friends who had come to bid them farewell. Tomos and Lisa stood silent with the rest, but an excitement ran through the company uniting them all, though many were strangers to one another.

Marged had insisted upon coming with Rowland to escort the first contingent of settlers all the way along the coast of Cardigan Bay to Milford Haven. When the voyagers were summoned on board the sailing vessel there was no need for further leave-taking. All the farewells had been said in Dolgellau. It now seemed as though the voyage had already started, and that the little party of Friends who remained on the quayside were already part of their past.

It was a grey day, clouds melting into the sea on the horizon, waves swelling impatiently, as if longing to be on the move, just as the travellers themselves were 'since it's going we are.'

Rowland watched the sails being hoisted aloft, the canvas unfurl and the slow movement of the vessel out of the harbour as if he were watching his own future. He realised there was no turning back now. Had he not known this from the start? His fate was aboard that ship, the mists swirling around her with a mysterious enchantment.

He felt Marged shiver at his side and saw the tears on her cheeks.

'No, no, don't my love,' he begged, taking her into his arms. 'They are going to a new life full of promise, and God is leading them.'

He looked into her eyes with an appeal for understanding. But, for once, her loneliness locked him out. When she spoke the words came from her with pain.

'The core of our people are aboard that ship . . . The loss . . . oh, the loss of it!'

The wind rushed from the sea to snatch up her words and scatter them over the harbour.